Cowboy at Heart

W9-CFK-002

SHIPMENT FIVE

Belonging to Bandera by Tina Leonard
Court Me, Cowboy by Barbara White Daille
His Best Friend's Bride by Jodi O'Donnell
The Cowboy's Return by Linda Warren
Baby Be Mine by Victoria Pade
The Cattle Baron by Margaret Way

SHIPMENT SIX

Crockett's Seduction by Tina Leonard
Coming Home to the Cattleman by Judy Christenberry
Almost Perfect by Judy Duarte
Cowboy Dad by Cathy McDavid
Real Cowboys by Roz Denny Fox
The Rancher Wore Suits by Rita Herron
Falling for the Texas Tycoon by Karen Rose Smith

SHIPMENT SEVEN

Last's Temptation by Tina Leonard
Daddy by Choice by Marin Thomas
The Cowboy, the Baby and the Bride-to-Be by Cara Colter
Luke's Proposal by Lois Faye Dyer
The Truth About Cowboys by Margot Early
The Other Side of Paradise by Laurie Paige

SHIPMENT EIGHT

Mason's Marriage by Tina Leonard
Bride at Briar's Ridge by Margaret Way
Texas Bluff by Linda Warren
Cupid and the Cowboy by Carol Finch
The Horseman's Son by Delores Fossen
Cattleman's Bride-to-Be by Lois Faye Dyer

**The rugged, masculine and independent men
of America's West know the value of hard work,
honor and family. They may be ranchers, tycoons
or the guy next door, but they are all cowboys at heart.
Don't miss any of the books in this collection!**

Cowboy
at
Heart

CROCKETT'S SEDUCTION
TINA
LEONARD
USA TODAY Bestselling Author

HARLEQUIN® COWBOY AT HEART

Recycling programs
for this product may
not exist in your area.

ISBN-13: 978-0-373-82633-9

CROCKETT'S SEDUCTION

Printed in U.S.A.

HARLEQUIN®
www.Harlequin.com

TINA LEONARD

is a *USA TODAY* bestselling and award-winning author of more than fifty projects, including several popular miniseries for Harlequin American Romance. Known for bad-boy heroes and smart, adventurous heroines, her books have made the *USA TODAY*, Waldenbooks, Ingram and Nielsen BookScan bestseller lists. Born on a military base, Tina lived in many states before eventually marrying the boy who did her crayon printing for her in the first grade. You can visit her at www.tinaleonard.com, or find her on Facebook and Twitter.

To Heather Diane Tipton, Marcy Shuler and Dawn Nelson, the quicker-picker-uppers, who pulled me out of the dumps. I loved having you in my office for "tea." What wonderful friends you are!

To all my Tina Leonard's Corral Gal Pals, for being awesome friends.

To the Scandalous Ladies, for recipes, reading and support you provide so generously.

Thank you, Stacy Boyd, for being a patient, encouraging editor. Kathleen Scheibling, bless you for your stalwart heart and patience.

Maggie Kelly, you are a gem.

Lisa and Dean, you have made my life fun!

Tim Leonard, my childhood best friend. I'm glad you did my homework in first grade.

Mother, I miss you. Judy, I miss you, too.

Shannon and Dad, what a wonderful blessing to have a wedding in the family. Welcome to the family, Shannon. We will take good care of you.

Chapter One

Sometimes she riled my temper, but she always made me smile.
—Maverick Jefferson to his sons after his
wife, Mercy, passed away

As Crockett Jefferson stood at his brother Bandera's wedding, he wondered if Valentine Cakes ever realized how much time he spent staring at her. He shouldn't. She was the mother of his brother Last's child. Crockett's deepest, darkest secret was that Valentine evoked fantasies in his mind, fantasies of the two of them laughing, touching, kissing—

"Well, that's that," his eldest brother, Mason, said looking to Hawk and Jellyfish, the amateur detectives and family friends who'd come to the Malfunction

Junction ranch to deliver news about Maverick Jefferson, the Jefferson brothers' missing father. Before he heard anything else about the mystery that obsessed Mason, Crockett once again found his vision glued to Valentine and her tiny daughter, Annette. His eyes had a habit they didn't want to give up, no matter how much family drama flowed around him.

Hawk looked at Mason. "Do you want to know what we learned about your father before or after you eat your piece of wedding cake?"

Crockett sighed, watching the fiery redhead as he heard the pronouncement about Maverick. With regret he took his gaze off Valentine. She held her daughter and a box of heart-shaped petits fours she'd made for Bandera's wedding reception. Being an artist of sorts, he appreciated both Valentine's lovely baked goods and her beauty. She smiled at him, her pretty blues eyes encouraging, her mouth bowing sweetly, and his heart turned over.

She could never know how he felt about her.

He didn't *want* to feel the way he did about the mother of his brother's child. So, to get away from the temptation to look at Valentine again, Crockett followed Hawk, Jellyfish and Mason to the shade of a tree so they could talk.

"We were able to confirm that Maverick was in Alaska, for a long time," Hawk said. "Your father lived with an Alaskan woman of Inuit descent. She found him slumped in a boat one day, floating offshore. Not knowing who he was or where he'd come from, she had friends help her carry him to her home. When he awakened, Maverick had no memory. She lived in a remote area, far from any town where a tourist group might have lost a member. Mannie kept him with her for four years, always hoping he might tell her something about himself."

Crockett looked at Mason, who surely

had to be feeling the same lead in the pit of his stomach that he was feeling. Finally, some trace of Maverick had been found, but he also feared there must be more to the story.

Jellyfish put a hand on Mason's shoulder. "You should know that Maverick only told Mannie a few things about himself, once some of his memory returned. She awakened one day to find him gone. He'd left behind food to keep her for a long time. Gifts, but not his heart. He was a natural wanderer. During the entire four years he'd stayed with her, she'd sensed he wasn't really with her by the distant look in his eyes when he searched the horizon."

"Oh, jeez," Crockett murmured. They were *all* wanderers. Right now, their father might still be out there somewhere, searching for what would ease his heart. Even with this new information they were not much closer to finding him.

"Maybe there is more to learn," Hawk said. "But we felt it was important to come back and tell you the news, then let you decide what more you want to know."

Crockett felt a deep tug in his chest. Now they would hold a family council to decide what to do. It was good they'd found out now, since all the brothers were at the ranch for the annual Fourth of July gathering and Bandera's wedding.

Now that so many of the Jefferson brothers had married and moved away, Mason wanted to hold a family reunion at least twice a year—Christmas in the winter and Fourth of July in the summer. Christmas was a natural choice, but Independence Day was a time when the pond was warm enough for the children to swim, Mason had said. But Crockett knew his request really had nothing to do with pond water. Mason just wanted the brothers and their families together at so-called Malfunction Junction ranch, their home.

Crockett had to admit there was something to the power of family bonding as he again watched Valentine help her tiny daughter across a field. Right now, he wanted to get away from all thoughts of family—and Maverick. It simply hurt too much to know that their father had been living on whale meat in a hut somewhere. It was life—but it wasn't life with them.

Could Maverick have been happy? Had he regained his memory? Or had he given up after their mother died? Crockett doubted they'd ever know all the answers. They'd been haunted for too many years by the questions, and each and every brother had learned various ways of dodging painful soul-searching.

"Thanks, guys," Crockett murmured to Hawk and Jellyfish since Mason seemed dumbstruck. "I'm sure Mason will call a family council after dinner to discuss what you told us. Stick around. Helga's made ribs, sweet peas and grilled corn, and I believe Valentine whipped up some blueberry pies. Comfort food is what we all could use right now. And good friends."

That said, he headed in Valentine's

direction. He grabbed the box of petits fours from her so that she could play with Annette. "Go on," he told Valentine. "You jump, too."

"Thank you, Crockett." Giving him a smile that tugged at his heart, Valentine pulled off her shoes and got inside the inflatable house-shaped structure. She bounced gently with her daughter.

With pleasure, he noted that all of Valentine bounced. Her hair, her breasts, even her laughter seemed to go up and down as she played with her daughter. He loved watching her be a mother.

Crockett lowered his head for a second, pushing his cowboy hat down. It was a shame that Valentine and his youngest brother, Last, had not worked out as a couple. They had a beautiful little daughter; Annette was such a sweet baby. And, wanting to support the new addition to the family, the Jefferson brothers had backed Valentine in her own business, a bakery she'd named Baked Valentines.

He would never have dreamed that the

one-time receptionist at a beauty salon would have been such a smart businesswoman—and an awesome baker. It was hard for him to understand why Last didn't love this talented, hardworking woman.... Boy, he was getting in a groove with being jealous of his brothers.

Lately, he'd found himself stewing over things he shouldn't. It was affecting the way he felt about his family.

First Calhoun, then Last.

Before his brother Calhoun had stolen Crockett's thunder and his creativity by becoming a better artist than him. Only more commercial, Calhoun always said, as if that made it more acceptable. Crockett had put his soul into painting. It had been a good life: cowboying by day, painting by night.

But he hadn't been able to paint in a long time. And now all he seemed to think about was Valentine.

The woman in question turned and fell over, laughing. Her jeans-clad bottom jiggled—and Crockett's artistic eye was transfixed.

He'd never seen anything with such rounded perfection. Bountiful and sexy. Lush and full.

"Only sculpting would do that form justice," he mused. "The warmth of fired clay, touched with the hue of a rosy—"

"What?" Valentine asked, sitting up to look at him. "Do you want to join us?"

His mind ablaze with creative thoughts, a new idea and a fierce desire to be near her, Crockett set the box of petits fours on the ground, pulled off his boots and got into the inflatable house. Annette giggled because he was unstable, not used to being on something jiggly, so he put his hands down and pushed on the floor to make her pop up and lose control, too.

Valentine playfully pushed back, catching him off guard. This time, it was Crockett who flew—right into her lap.

Oh, God, she felt good. She was every bit as soft as she looked, and even better, she smelled like cinnamon. Her smile faded as she stared down at him, seeing something in his eyes he didn't want her to see.

Bad, bad timing.

Rolling away, he rose to his feet. Valentine watched him, her smile completely gone now, her gaze questioning.

He was going to ruin a good friendship with his curiosity about Valentine. Curiosity? That was a shifty word for what he now realized was full-blown desire.

He was on a path toward certain heartbreak.

VALENTINE WATCHED AS Crockett exited the inflatable house. He put his hat on, tipping the brim to her, and touched one finger to Annette's small hand. Then he left.

Just like that. Gone.

Had he thought she was flirting with him? Something miserably like rejection seeped through her—an experience she'd had all too often recently, every time she came into accidental contact with Last.

She didn't know what she would have

done without the other Jefferson brothers. In her heart, she knew Last was a good man—he was very good to Annette. But there was always that wall of discomfort between them, and she'd really relied on the kindness of his brothers to make her feel less awkward.

She had been determined to make good in their eyes, to show them that she wasn't the bad girl she'd been. Her sister Nina had made a wonderful marriage to Navarro Jefferson. Navarro and Nina were so happy on their land up North that sometimes Valentine was tempted to follow them up there. She would love to be near her sister, and she would love for Annette to be able to know her aunt and uncle.

What held her in Union Junction, Texas, quite simply, was Last. Although he hadn't started out as the world's best dad, he had begun a relationship with Annette that Valentine believed would strengthen and grow over the years. Annette seemed to know that Last was her special man, her daddy, among all the Jefferson brothers who came and went. There was a different sparkle in her eyes when she asked to be held by Last.

So Valentine stayed, though she knew Last would never be comfortable around *her*.

It was Mason who'd had faith in her, and he'd helped her turn her life around. She took a job at the bakery in town soon after Annette's birth, and what started out as a way to gain monetary independence blossomed into true love. She was an artist of a different kind. Beautiful baked goods, lovingly crafted. Her reputation for beauty spread throughout Union Junction, and when the owner decided to sell out, it was Mason who had gone to the brothers and suggested that they back Valentine as the new owner.

She would never forget the moment the Jefferson brothers had told her of their gift, to her and to Annette. Her self-worth had been validated for the first time in her life, and she knew she would do anything to show them that she was a different woman from the one who had come to them pregnant and bringing a paternity lawsuit aimed at taking money from their family.

Now, her gaze followed Crockett as he strode away. She sighed. The Jeffersons had been far too good to her. It was ridiculous for her to want anything more than friendship from the good-looking, gentle cowboy.

"Unfortunately," she told Annette, scooping her daughter into her lap, "everything in my life should stay just as it is, the best it's ever been."

Annette looked up at her with a smile, her chubby fingers reaching out to her mom. "One day," Valentine told Annette, "one day I'll find my real prince. And he won't bear the last name of Jefferson."

She lightly bounced Annette some more, but the one thing that no lighthearted playing could cure was the ache she'd felt when Crockett had so suddenly walked away.

Chapter Two

It unnerved Crockett how much he thought about Valentine. He was living in a fool's world, dreaming the impossible dream.

He could hear the gossip in Union Junction now: "Yes, Crockett Jefferson's twin, Navarro, married Nina, then Crockett went and married Valentine, Nina's sister. *And* she's the mother of Last Jefferson's child. That's one of the many reasons we call that ranch Malfunction Junction!"

Definitely a fool's world. He wished Valentine's sweet face and trusting eyes didn't haunt him.

The only cure for thoughts a man couldn't control was to busy himself with something that needed to be fixed. In this case, Crockett decided, what most needed fixing was himself.

There had to be room for two artists in the family. So the day after Bandera's wedding, the day after Mason had sent Hawk and Jellyfish back out to look for Maverick, the day after most of his married brothers had left the ranch, he sat in front of a canvas in a quiet attic hideaway at the main ranch house, staring with determination at the empty white board in front of him. A tube of ochre tempted him to begin something warm and vibrant. But he couldn't make his fingers pick up the tube.

His soul wanted to create, but his mind wanted to think about Valentine. His creativity was hiding from the chaos.

"Whatcha doing, Uncle Crockett?" a young voice asked as Kenny crawled through the attic hole to stare at him. "Dad wants your help fixing our windmill. It has a squeak in its turn."

"Dad" was Crockett's brother Calhoun,

the significant drain on Crockett's creativity.

"Hey, Kenny," Crockett said, not surprised when Kenny's big sister Minnie crawled up behind her brother. "And, Miss Minnie."

"Hi, Uncle Crockett." She stood beside his chair and squinted at the blank canvas. "Gonna get started soon? Or are you pondering?"

"Pondering."

He loved Calhoun's kids, but right now, he wished they hadn't brought their inquisitiveness into his sanctuary. It was the only place he'd thought of where his nosy brothers might not figure out what he was up to. He needed to create in peace. If he was lucky, it would all come back to him—and then he could keep his wandering mind off Valentine.

Minnie looked at him sympathetically. "Dad's been painting some portraits of Widow Fancy. She wanted some for her grandkids."

Crockett nodded. "That's nice."

"Maybe you could draw our windmill. Or our horse," Kenny added. "Gypsy would love to be painted."

"She is an old show pony," Crockett agreed. "But you can get Calhoun to do that for you."

"Nah," Minnie said. "Mama says you're the real artist in the family."

Crockett perked up. "Really? Olivia says that about me?"

"Yeah." Minnie nodded. "She says you're all moody and soulful, and surely that equates to great talent just waiting to be sprung." Minnie sighed dramatically. "Of course, Dad says it's not your talent that needs to be sprung, it's your drawers."

"Yeah," Kenny said. "We can't understand what's wrong with your drawers. Are they stuck? I sure hope it's not your sock drawer," he said. "You won't like wearing boots without socks. One time I did that, and I had blisters—"

"Kenny," Crockett interrupted kindly. "Minnie, would the two of you run and tell your father that I will be happy to help him fix the windmill?"

They nodded solemnly.

"I'll be down there sometime this afternoon. But I need the two of you to do me a favor," he said, making his tone conspiratorial.

"Okay," Minnie whispered.

"Please don't tell Calhoun or anybody else that I was up here or that I was painting."

"*Thinking* about painting," Kenny reminded him. "You haven't painted anything yet."

Crockett sighed at his childish honesty. "True. Off you go, both of you, and remember, this is our secret. Only the two of you know where to find me."

"Okay." Minnie's eyes shone. "We're great at keeping secrets!"

He thought about the jibe that Calhoun probably hadn't meant for his kids to overhear and repeat. "I know you are," he said. "Thanks."

They hugged him, then carefully descended the ladder.

"Hey, kids," Crockett heard someone say. He froze as he recognized Valentine's voice. "What are you two doing up there?"

His heart seemed to stop beating as he waited for Minnie and Kenny to reply. He did not want Valentine to visit the one place where he could hide out and try to paint her out of his memory.

"We were looking for something," Minnie said. "It's kind of dusty up there, though, and there's not anything interesting."

He grimaced. More honesty.

"Attics are fun to look through," Valentine said. "My sister and I used to have an attic. Here, let me help you close it."

Crockett heard the stairs fold, then boom! The attic door closed, securely locking him away with his floundering creativity.

"Wonderful," he grumbled, feeling more moody and soulful than ever.

Quickly, he strode to the window, looking down into the yard. He was rewarded by the sight of Valentine walking with Kenny and Minnie across the lawn.

He loved looking at Valentine. Okay, so maybe he was spying, but she was so feminine that he even enjoyed watching her walk away.

Just then, Minnie turned around, her little face tipped up in his direction. Very discreetly, she waved.

He jumped away from the window, his heart beating hard. *Too close.* He had to stop getting funky over that little package of female dynamite. *Back to my creation.*

After a long fruitless period of staring at the blank canvas, his cell phone rang, startling him out of his churning thoughts. "Hello?"

"Crockett, it's Calhoun. Minnie says you're going to help me with the windmill."

"Yeah," Crockett said reluctantly, knowing that Valentine had walked the kids home. She would be at Calhoun's house. Even if he didn't want to avoid her, which he did, he was trapped in the attic. The biggest problem of the two was Valentine, hands down. "Not right now," he said.

"When?" Calhoun asked. "Valentine's here. Olivia says she'll whip up some barbecue if you want to head this way. She's going to teach Valentine how to ride Gypsy after supper."

That would be worth seeing, but he knew he shouldn't see it. "Tell Olivia thanks, but I can't do it, dude."

"Why?"

"I'm busy," Crockett said. "Look for me tomorrow." He snapped the phone off and sat in front of his canvas again, trying to gather his scattered thoughts.

Then it came to him. He should start easy, with a warm-up. Nothing difficult. Something that would waken his muse and loosen up his inner artist.

A small challenge would totally keep his mind off Valentine and how she would look while learning to ride the cagey

Gypsy. A still life would keep him from sitting here thinking about how all of Valentine seemed to bounce so cutely whenever she…well, bounced.

A pear would be the perfect thing to paint. "A pear in a bowl," he murmured. "*Very* still."

Slowly, his hand unsure, he trailed his first colored stroke against the empty whiteness.

"It's supposed to be supernatural," Crockett heard someone whisper. "Don't you get it?"

"I think it's extraterrestrial maybe." The voice sounded puzzled. "Could be a heart, Van Gogh style. With something cut off. Wasn't Van Gogh famous for cutting things off?"

"I don't quite see that," came the quiet reply. "I think it's a woman's buttocks."

Crockett's eyes snapped open. Last and Mason were standing over him, staring at his painting. He jumped to his feet. "What the hell?" he demanded, trying to cover his precious secret from their puzzled glances.

"Sorry," Mason said. "We sent out a search team for you when you didn't hit the table for supper. It's not like you to miss a meal."

"Nope," Last said, his eyes huge. "What the hell is that thing you painted? And why are you up here, hiding out with the dust bunnies?"

"So you wouldn't bug me," Crockett snapped. "And I wish I'd stayed hidden. I'm feeling very intruded upon."

Last's eyes widened. "We were worried about you."

"Entirely unnecessary." He'd just gotten tired and had decided to stretch out and rest his eyes. "How'd you find me up here?"

Mason shrugged. "There's all kinds of dirt on the floor from the attic door being opened. I don't guess anybody's been up here in ages. We really ought to clean it out." Glancing around, he sighed. "When we have time."

"So, what did you paint?" Last said. "Mason thinks it's a Picasso-style heart—"

"Van Gogh," Mason corrected.

"I'm thinking the red tones are sexual," Last said. "The curves are feminine and delicate, so it's probably a woman's fanny. It almost reminds me of Georgia O'Keeffe. You know how she revealed the sexual nature of women when she painted those petals." Last scratched his head as he looked at his brother. "But you never think about sex when you're holding a paintbrush. I probably just didn't get your vision. Let me have another look."

"No!" Crockett hopped away with his overcritiqued treasure. Gently, he set it down where it could dry in peace. "Look, do you guys mind getting the hell out?"

"No problem, Picasso," Mason said. "But since it seems your creativity has fizzled for the moment, you think we could get you to come down for supper?"

"Why not?" Crockett said, following them down the stairs. "I have nothing better to do than be harassed by my brothers."

"Excellent." Mason headed into the kitchen, then sat at the table and tucked a napkin into his lap. "Helga cooked a wonderful meal."

He beamed, delighted that Mimi didn't borrow the housekeeper so much now that Mimi lived in town. With a smaller place and with her daughter being older, things were going more smoothly for Mimi.

Except for her cockamamy idea of running for sheriff, with Mason as deputy, an idea that Crockett knew Mason opposed. It was no job for a woman, Mason had said, especially a woman like Mimi.

The brothers had rolled their eyes, ignoring Mason. Mimi would do whatever the heck Mimi wanted—and Mason would no doubt find himself neck-deep in Mimi-schemies.

"It's delicious, Helga," Crockett said to the housekeeper. Actually, now that he was eating, he was glad his brothers had rescued him from his upstairs jail.

He had gotten hungry. And now that he'd survived their mockery and realized they hadn't made as much fun of his first attempt at painting as he'd feared, he was feeling almost good about his dysfunctional family.

And then the door opened and Valentine walked in with Olivia, Calhoun and the kids.

"Ah, just in time for dinner," Calhoun said, grinning as he helped his kids and Olivia onto the plank seats.

Crockett stared, all his contentment shriveling. "I thought you were eating at your house."

"Yeah, but Helga called and said she'd made extra, and why didn't we come on up? So here we are," Calhoun said.

Yes, here they were, Crockett thought, before remembering his manners. He stood and pushed the plank seat back a bit so Valentine could more comfortably seat herself. Beside him, of course, because the table was then balanced with an equal number of people on each side.

Helga quickly handed out extra plates, but Crockett's creativity and hunger left all at once, replaced by a different kind of need.

He suddenly realized the delicate floral scent he smelled was coming from Valentine. He quickly drank some water. She looked at him, her smile somehow unsure, and he put the glass down.

Across the table, Last watched them curiously. Minnie and Kenny ate happily, and Annette sat in her father's lap, grinning as she dug her fingers into Last's mashed potatoes.

Tension spread through Crockett. He turned his attention back to the food he couldn't eat.

"In case you're wondering what's in that box on the counter," Valentine said when the silence at the table grew long, "it's a cake for Mason."

"Really? That was nice of you, Valentine," Mason replied sincerely. "We love your cakes."

Valentine beamed, clearly pleased with the compliment. "It's a birthday cake someone ordered for you, a secret admirer," Valentine said. "I didn't know it was your birthday."

Crockett turned his attention back to Valentine, relieved that he had a reason to look at her.

"It's not my birthday," Mason said, frowning. "It's not any of our birthdays."

The smile slid from Valentine's face, and Crockett felt sorry for her.

"Oh," she said softly.

"Who sent it?" Last asked.

"She paid cash," Valentine said. "She just said she was a secret admirer. I thought you knew her." A becoming blush spread across her delicate cheeks. "I'll take the cake back."

"No way," Mason said. "I never give up cake." He took the box from Helga.

"Mason, no," Valentine said. "Believe me, you do not want this cake."

"Mmm, chocolate," Mason said, cutting off a big piece. "Plates for everyone, please, Helga."

Then Mason stopped, looking confused. Crockett could feel Valentine shifting nervously on the bench, as if she wanted to get up and flee.

Mason lifted a thong from the center of the cake. "What's this?"

Last started laughing. Olivia hid a smile. Minnie and Kenny were agog, and Annette pushed mashed potatoes into her hair happily while the adults' attention was elsewhere.

"The lady said she'd just been to Victoria's Secret and wanted to send you something you liked almost as much as chocolate," Valentine said.

She sounded on the verge of tears, so Crockett put an arm around her shoulders, giving her a squeeze. To his surprise, she hid her face against his chest. It was only for a second, but it was enough to send an arrow of joy quivering straight into his heart.

"Oh, well," Mason said. "I can't imagine who sent it, but since you baked it, I won't let a thong stop me from eating a delicious Baked Valentine. If you think about it, this brings a whole new meaning to the name of your store, Valentine."

Crockett knew Mason was trying to make Valentine feel better by making her laugh, but she was too embarrassed. "It's okay," Crockett told her. "We get stuff like that all the time."

The second he said it, he wished he hadn't. Valentine pulled away from him. She took Annette from Last and started to wipe the potatoes off the baby's fingers and from her hair.

"Nice going, Leonardo da Vinci," Mason said to Crockett, slapping a piece of cake in front of him. "Now Valentine thinks we're a bunch of panty-collecting apes."

Helga used a pair of tongs to snag the offending missive off the table and toss it in the trash. "Bad girls."

Silence fell.

"Don't be upset, Valentine," Olivia finally said. "The cake is wonderful. And so pretty, too."

"Thank you," Valentine said softly.

"I'm sorry to have to call it a night in the middle of dinner, but Annette's managed to get potatoes mashed into her diapers. I'm going to take her on home."

They all stood, trying to get her to stay. Helga offered to rinse the baby at the sink, and Last said a bit of potatoes wasn't going to hurt Annette. But Valentine thanked Helga for dinner and said good-night, not really looking at any of them.

The front door closed, and Crockett looked at Mason. "Sorry. I was trying to make her feel better."

"I don't think it worked." Mason sat down, licking the frosting from his fingers. "I have to say, she bakes so much better than the folks who used to own the store. This is *good.*"

It was more than Crockett could stand, thinking about Valentine walking to her little house on the far side of the ranch, alone and upset. If Last wasn't going to get up to walk her home, then Crockett would.

"I'll be right back," he said, hurrying out the door.

Valentine heard boots coming after her, and her heart jumped when she recognized Crockett's voice. Oh, she didn't want to talk to him now. Once he'd admitted that he and his brothers frequently received favors like panties from women, she had known she had to leave. The thought that one day she might take an order like that for Crockett made her whole inner being turn cold with some emotion she'd never felt before, an emotion she didn't understand and wanted to get away from, quickly.

"Wait up," Crockett said, swooping Annette from her arms. "The night's still young, even for this tater-stealing spud."

"Spud needs a bath and a bedtime story."

"I don't like the nickname *Spud. Tater* sounds a lot more feminine," Crockett protested, his teasing voice trying to wheedle a smile from Valentine. "Give your uncle a kiss, Tater."

Valentine appreciated his effort, but she couldn't smile. He didn't know how ragged her heart felt.

"Don't be embarrassed about all that back there," Crockett said. "It was the best thing that could happen to Mason. He's getting way too stodgy. Didn't you see how happy he was?"

"I'm sure he thinks it's weird that I baked it for him. But I honestly thought she knew him and that maybe there was some shared history between them."

"Nah," Crockett said easily. "Mason's never shared much history with anyone, except Mimi, and I'm not sure their history has anything to do with panties. Mimi would be more likely to leave Mason's drawers in a tree somewhere for all the world to see."

Valentine slowly smiled. "She wouldn't."

"She would. There is no limit to the fun we call Mimi."

She gave Crockett a sidelong glance. "Do you have any history?"

"The kind where someone orders me

a specially baked cake with lingerie filling? No. Not unless you want to order me
one." He gave her a devilish wink that
made her heart race restlessly. "Bras,
panties, it doesn't matter. I'm not as picky
as Mason."

"I don't know what temperature I'd
have to put the oven on to bake a bra into
a cake."

"Hot, hot, hot," Crockett said, kissing
Tater on her head as he held her.

Valentine felt a blush steal over her
cheeks. "Give me the spud," she said.
"We are late for a rub-a-dub in the tub."
She took Annette from Crockett, amazed
by the warmth of his body as her arms
brushed his. Hot, hot, hot was right. Cau-
tiously, she glanced over Annette's head,
peeping at the big cowboy. "Good night,
Uncle Crockett," she said, waving Annette's little fist.

"I could come in and make soap carv-
ings for her," Crockett offered. "It's something I learned in Maverick's boot camp."

It was tempting, but Valentine knew

too well that she had no business allowing herself to accept such an invitation. She and Crockett needed to stay separate, on the ranch and in their lives.

Annette started to fuss, giving Valentine an excuse to shake her head. "Thanks. Another time. Good night, Crockett." She walked inside her house, then turned to wave one last goodbye.

He stood there, his arms crossed over his chest and his legs spread as he watched her, the very essence of sexiness and protectiveness. Everything that was female inside her electrified and went on red alert.

He tipped his hat to her.

Slowly, she backed away from the door, closing it behind her. Her pulse thundered. He was hotter than a man had a right to be.

"You like him," she whispered to Annette as they walked down the hall, "and so do I."

The flattered feelings Crockett gave her were like a sweet, forbidden confection—one an unwise woman ate and then later regretted.

Valentine might have made mistakes in her past, but this time she would be wise. If she didn't lose her head, then she couldn't lose her heart.

Chapter Three

If Crockett hadn't been thinking about panty-filled cakes and how pretty Valentine's fanny probably looked in a thong, he might have noticed Last waiting for him on the porch.

"Bro," Last said, his arms crossed over his chest. "It seems strange to me that your creativity has returned, and now you're walking Valentine home. It's like...I don't know. One and one makes two, you know?"

Crockett frowned, walking around his brother. "Seems to me the math's already been done. One and one made three. You didn't choose to walk two parts of the equation home, so shut the hell up."

Last followed him into the house. "That doesn't mean you should have."

"Then who, Last?" Crockett put his hat on the counter and stared his brother down. "It was a courtesy, nothing more, one which you should have performed."

Last shrugged. "At the table, it seemed like you two were getting along pretty well."

Crockett sighed. "Are you trying to tell me that you have feelings for her? That you *ever* had feelings for her?"

"Not *those* kind of feelings."

Crockett breathed a sigh of relief that he didn't allow his brother to hear.

"But Annette's my daughter."

Crockett shook his head. "I thought I had all the jealousy in the family."

"I've got my fair share."

They sat down on the sofa, glancing around to make sure Helga wasn't around before putting their boots on the coffee table.

"I'm just getting good at the relationship with my daughter," Last said quietly. "Frankly, it took me a while."

"I know. We thought your Mohawk phase might last longer than it did." Crockett picked up the remote and began channel surfing. Some things were easier to discuss lightly.

"Maybe I shouldn't have brought it up," Last said. "I just wanted you to know how I feel."

Crockett nodded and closed his eyes, wishing Last would cool his jets. Family angst wasn't what he wanted to think about. He wanted to think about Valentine—and her fanny—and about the creative ideas suddenly filling his mind. Something about that tiny woman with the very round, very upstanding tushie made his juices flow, made him want to… sculpt. *Her.*

She brought inspiration to life inside him in ways he had never imagined. What medium would best illustrate her curves?

Clay! Calhoun didn't work with clay!

"I need some more time to work things out with Valentine."

Last's words penetrated the dense fog of Crockett's inspired musing. "I wasn't aware the two of you were trying to work anything out."

"Not like that," Last admitted. "It's the family angle I'm working on. The father thing."

A curious rush of jealousy, more powerful than anything Crockett had experienced before, surprised him. "Father thing?"

"Yeah, I've been polishing my game. Performing my obligations. Whatever you want to call it."

"Let me get this straight. From the day Frisco Joe met Annabelle and her baby, Emmie, you talked about Jefferson children. You sent all our brothers off with marching orders to procreate. Surprise, surprise, you become a dad, too, only you get mad as hell and do everything you can to ignore Annette for months, leaving your responsibilities to Mason and me and our other brothers. *Now* you decide to bust my chops because I'm paying attention to Valentine and Annette?" He shook his head. "Dude, it's not going to work. You can't treat people that way. You've ignored Valentine since she came to the ranch. I'm not trying to get in your way when it comes to being a dad, but you're not going to get in my way of…whatever."

"And what is whatever? Just so I'll understand."

Crockett slapped his brother on the back of the head. "She's a nice lady. I like to look at her."

Last moved away from his older brother's reach. "And if I don't like *whatever?* If I need more time to get my own deal worked out with my family? Then what?"

"Have at it." He looked his brother in the eyes. "Don't get competitive, Last. You don't like hanging around her, I do. Deal with it."

Last got up from the couch, agony on his face. "I am trying to be as good a father as Maverick was."

"I'm not stopping you."

Last sighed. "I feel like I need something that's mine, where none of my brothers overshadow me."

Crockett could relate to that feeling. "We're just friends. And I'm only interested in spending time with her because it seems I've recently turned into a butt-man."

"Butt-*head,* you mean."

"No, butt-man. Valentine has a great tush. It inspires my creativity. That's all I'm thinking about. Nothing deeper than that."

Last nodded, then left Crockett with the TV while he headed down to Valentine's. He hesitated before knocking on the door. Crockett was pretty much correct: Last had avoided Valentine for a long time.

The realization that he was a father had changed his life and frightened him. He'd doubted his ability to be a proper role model. He hadn't wanted to be tied down to a woman. At the time, it had felt as if he'd gotten roped in. Later, he realized that the few pounds of squealing flesh that bore his name wasn't all that frightening. He'd slowly begun to worm his way into Valentine's good graces, and he'd moved just as slowly over the first bumps of fatherhood.

He'd been feeling pretty good about matters—until Crockett had started eyeing his family.

The door opened and Valentine looked out at him. "Hi, Last," she said, her tone somewhat surprised.

Of course she was surprised. "Is Annette asleep?"

"Nearly. Did you want to see her?"

He shifted. "Actually, I wanted to ask you something."

Her big eyes widened. "All right."

"There's never going to be anything between you and me, is there?"

Valentine was so shocked by Last coming to her house and asking her this question that it took her a second to shake her head. "I think we're better off as friends. You don't want more than that, do you?"

"I want to be first in my daughter's life."

"And you're worried that you won't be?" This was a side of Last she'd never seen before.

"Maybe."

"Last, Annette knows who you are," Valentine said softly. "That should be reassurance enough."

"Yeah." He backed away from the door. "Okay."

Valentine took a deep breath. "For what it's worth, Last, I never set out to trap you with fatherhood. If you avoid me because you think I'm after you, it's not true. I don't remember much about our night together, but I know it got out of hand pretty quick and that neither of us were ourselves. Nor were either of us under any delusions."

He looked grim. "Sometimes I wonder if it really happened."

"I know."

His mouth settled into a tense line. "I think, Valentine, I owe you an apology.

I had some wildness in me, and I never thought about the consequences of my actions. For either of us, but especially for you."

Valentine smiled slightly. "Thank you. But it doesn't matter anymore. We have a daughter we both love."

"We sure do." For the first time, he smiled. "I'm still kind of amazed that I'm a dad."

"Scary?"

"Scary, but awesome." He stepped down off the porch. "By the way, do you have a thing for my brother Crockett?"

Her smile slipped, and she gave him a warning glare. "Haven't you asked the one question you came here to ask?"

He laughed and put up his hands in mock surrender. "All right."

She opened the door. "I have to get to work early in the morning."

He nodded. "Good night."

"Good night." Closing the door, Valentine wondered which of Last's questions he'd really come to ask. She'd never know—but one thing she did know, she had a thing for Crockett.

OKAY, SO IT WAS WRONG to be hiding in the bushes. Crockett knew that. But he wasn't so much hiding as skulking, he figured, in the old-time manner any villain from a black-and-white movie would appreciate.

But what else could a man do? The second he'd realized Last had a major burr under his saddle and was heading down to Valentine's house, Crockett had to tag along to eavesdrop.

He'd heard everything, amazed that Valentine and Last spoke with each other so easily about such a difficult subject. And how dare Last ask her if she had a thing for him? Crockett was just honest enough to admit his ears had stretched out about a foot to hear her reply, his heart hoping for an affirmative answer of some sort.

Well, he hadn't gotten an affirmative, but he hadn't overheard a negative, either. Wasn't that a good sign?

He untangled himself from the bushes and headed back toward the main house. Half of him wanted to go pound Last for muddying the waters; he'd have to keep an eye on that brother of his. But right now the other half of him wanted to express his joy.

She didn't say that she didn't *have a thing for me,* he repeated to himself happily.

IN MIMI'S TOWNHOUSE the next day Mimi and Mason were seated at the kitchen table drinking tea and glaring at each other. Mimi's daughter, Nanette, sat in Mason's lap, playing with a doll he'd given her, completely oblivious to the tension in the room.

"I don't want to be your deputy," Mason said. "It's a harebrained idea, as usual."

"Sometimes you like my ideas," she reminded him.

Mason wondered if he'd truly liked her ideas, or if he'd simply been driven by the inner devil that sometimes took the wheel of the Jefferson boys. "I may have lost my sense of direction and allowed you to lead me astray a time or two."

"So you don't want to be my deputy because of the news about Maverick?" Mimi asked. "Are you leaving to look for him again?"

"No." He kissed the top of Nanette's head, drawing peace from her presence. "It wouldn't do me any good. Hawk and Jellyfish can find whatever is out there. They're the trackers. Me, I'm just a farm boy."

She laughed. "Right."

"So."

Taking a sip of tea, he considered Mimi. She was just as pretty as she'd ever been. Maybe even prettier. He supposed that now that she was officially divorced from Brian, men would flock to her door. That thought rattled him quite a bit more than it should. So he thought about Nanette instead. She needed a stable male influence in her life. She had Mimi's father, the sheriff, of course. And Barley, Calhoun's father-in-law, who came around often to play checkers and carouse with the sheriff a bit. And all the Jefferson brothers did their part for their former neighbor, because they loved Mimi like a sister and adored Nanette like one of their own.

But was it enough? "I may take Nanette to the park today."

Mimi's brows raised. "She'd like that."

"Yeah." He'd like it, too. He liked spending time with this child. Maybe he felt sorry for her since her father was never around. One thing Mimi'd had while growing up—wild March hare that she was—was the stable influence of the sheriff.

Nanette was a baby, really, but she still needed at least one man who cared about her in a…fatherly way.

He decided it was up to him. "Yeah, the deputy thing isn't for me. And now that the sheriff has nearly gotten over the liver infection, can he keep his post?"

Mimi shook her head. "He can't run for

sheriff again. Dad really needs to take it easy. He's happy here in town, too, more than I thought he'd be." She sighed. "Although I will admit I never thought we'd leave our little farm."

Mason was just glad they hadn't moved farther away. With Mimi, you could never tell what might happen. "Ever hear from Brian?"

"No. Not really. He still does some paperwork for Dad."

"Ah." Mason felt the tiny stab of jealousy inside him recede. He supposed he'd always been a bit worried that Mimi and Brian might work things out. It was so wrong of him to be happy that their marriage had failed! What kind of friend was he?

"You know, Mason," Mimi said, "that little bundle of joy you're holding is what gave my father the will to live. I think he fought that infection with every shred of strength he had in him just to see her grow up."

"Miracle girl." Mason kissed the top

of her head again. "Don't start thinking you're special, though, toot."

Nanette patted his face, then pretended to steal his nose.

"Okay, off to the park we go. You want to come?"

Mimi shook her head. "Thanks. You go on."

Mason gathered Nanette in his arms then turned to look at Mimi. "I don't think you should run for sheriff, either. It's too dangerous. You need to think of your little girl."

"And I've decided to take your advice on that matter. Of course, your horsey opinion doesn't have anything to do with my change of mind, but I have thought long and hard on it. You're right."

Mason was shocked. "Is that a first?"

Mimi laughed. "Hell, yes, so don't be annoying and gloat."

"Humph." He thought about her capitulation and wondered aloud, "What else could I get out of you while you're in this easy mood? One ought to grab all the candy while the store's open and free, I think."

"I'm not exactly candy," Mimi said.

No, but she *was* being sweet. He frowned. "Mimi," he said, "have you ever thought about the fact that sometimes you and I really get along?"

Chapter Four

Hidden in the attic that he had accepted as his artistic loft, Crockett stared at the clay lump in front of him. This was definitely a new playground. Clay didn't have the color of paints, or the lightness of spirit that said, "Create freely!"

But the lump represented wonderful opportunities. It gave him a chance to think about the new him. Sculptor. Artist of a molding medium. He worked the clay between his fingers. He had eschewed white, opting to start with red clay. Would he enjoy making something without a brush? He hoped he didn't become frustrated or miss the sensation of a brush sliding across canvas.

"I have a barn to clean out, so you and

I better come to terms," he told the lump. "Be beautiful."

"Crockett?" a voice called up the stairs.

Valentine! Blast! "Yes?"

"Can I talk to you for a second?"

So much for having a secret lair. Had someone put out a sign when he wasn't looking? *This way to Crockett's cave?* But if someone had to bother him he was glad it was Valentine. She was worth a break.

"Sure. Come on up."

She appeared at the top of the ladder, and he reached to help her into the room. "This space is nice."

He glanced around. "Not really."

"Oh, sure. This is the perfect place to read a book! Especially on a rainy day." She smiled, giving a fake shiver. "A cold, rainy day."

"It's July. Hard to think about cold, rainy days."

"Yeah. You know, you just need a window seat up here, a fresh coat of paint, and this place would be a wonderful studio."

Of course, she was right, but he didn't want her redecorating his hideout. Ugly and in some disarray, it suited his mood. "Hey, what's up, anyway? What brings you to the dustiest part of the ranch?"

She turned to look out the window, which he appreciated, because he could now evaluate her curves. Yes, she was just as he remembered: full and feminine and made for a man who appreciated round, apple-shaped—

"You're making me self-conscious, Crockett," Valentine said, laughing. "You always seem to be staring at my fanny."

"Your jeans fit good," he said. "I've never known Wrangler jeans to fit anyone quite like yours fit you."

"And you would be a connoisseur of fannies," she teased.

"Purely a statement of truth." Valentine was hotter than a pistol, in his book—but it was a book he wasn't going to read, window seat and fresh paint or not. "So once again, what do you want?"

She took a deep breath. "I was going to see what you thought about me having a special little 'do' here for Father's Day."

He stopped fiddling with the lump of clay. "Father's Day? That was last month."

"Yes. Well there are rather a lot of fathers around here. And we didn't have a real celebration for them. Last, the sheriff, Barley, Calhoun—"

He scowled at his brothers' names. "You're doing this for Last."

"I would like to do something for him," Valentine admitted. "I think he would enjoy being celebrated as a father. He has really been good to Annette."

He guessed late was better than never. "Have you mentioned this party idea to Mason?"

"Not yet. I thought I'd speak to you first."

"Why me? I'm not a father." A fact he hated to admit, for some reason. Why wasn't he a father? Because he hadn't gone on a hootenanny and gotten someone pregnant as Last had, he supposed. But that route to fatherhood seemed unappealing when there were other ways.

Like with Valentine.

The thought swept over him before he could stop it. Valentine made beautiful babies; she made beautiful everything.

"I like to talk to you about whatever's on my mind," she said simply. "You're reasonable."

Reasonable was the last thing he was feeling. "I'm not a father," he repeated, "but it sounds like something my brothers, at least, would enjoy. Can I come if I'm not a father?"

She looked at him. "Why do you keep saying that?"

"I don't know. It could be bothering me."

They stared at each other for a long time, and the silence felt awkward.

"Do you want to be a father?" Valentine asked softly.

Crockett eased back on his stool. "You seem happy being a parent."

She smiled. "Yes, I love being a mother. But I am a parent of one. I'm not having any more children, so the burden doesn't seem overly large."

His brows rose, and an uncomfortable feeling lodged in his stomach. "You're never having any more kids?"

She shrugged. "I'm a single mother. It's rewarding, but enough of a struggle that I know I don't plan on having more children."

"I think Annette would like a little brother to drag around."

"I think she has plenty of people wrapped in the crook of her finger." She sat down across from him. "So about the party."

"Yeah," Crockett said reluctantly, realizing he wouldn't enjoy watching his brother get kudos for being a dad. "Sounds like a real wingding."

He scratched his head. His brain disliked the notion of Valentine not having more children. It didn't sit right with him. Why? He drummed his fingers, then cracked his knuckles—and then it hit him.

He *really* wanted a child.

He rolled the very foreign thought around in his mind again. Prickles ran across his scalp. Valentine eyed him with a concerned gaze.

"Are you all right? You've gone quite pale." She moved closer to examine him. She smelled fresh. "No, you're definitely pale. Crockett, is something wrong?"

Well, hell, yeah. He wanted a baby. He wanted a baby, more specifically, with her, the last person on earth he should be thinking about.

Yeah, something was very definitely out of whack. He was all screwed up. "I need to be alone."

"Oh." Valentine pulled away from him. "All right." She walked across to the ladder before turning to say, "So you think it would be all right to approach Mason about the belated Father's Day picnic?"

"Yeah. Sure." He returned his gaze to the lump in front of him. With a sigh, he designated himself an oaf and told himself not to abuse Valentine's kindness. "Hey, he'll probably be all over it."

Valentine smiled. "Thanks, Crockett."

"Bye."

She waved and headed downstairs. He told his baby thoughts and the rise in his Levi's that always seemed to accompany Valentine to be gone. Snatching the clay from its mooring, he reviewed it. He would start out small and see where it would go.

A COUPLE OF HOURS LATER he had a rounded booty that was completely Valentine. Okay, so he still needed to work on the rest of the body, but the reclining piece had legs that flowed sweetly into a curving backside. The knees lay against each other in a position that was feminine and yet somehow sexual.

He liked the feeling of clay between his fingers, he decided, and the satisfaction of creating something from mere dirt. "Sweet," he said. "Not too shabby for a beginner."

Beyond the curving posterior, he needed a torso and head. But he'd think about that later. For now, the piece that had been teasing his brain was complete.

He covered his artwork and headed down the stairs. His passion had finally been lit again. His creativity was stoked after many months of lying quiet, like a banked fire. This could not be taken from him. None of his brothers sculpted. If he moved his lair somewhere else, everything would be perfect. He could work in total peace and quiet, without his brothers' do-drop-in interruptions.

Speaking of interruptions… He was almost out the door when he saw Last waving at him. "Great," he said, "here comes Mr. Father's Day himself."

Last jogged over and gave Crockett a pop on the arm. "Where have you been?"

"In none-of-your-business-land," Crockett said pointedly. "Are you writing a book?"

"No. Do you have a second?"

"Is it a second in real time, or Last time?"

"Real time." Last looked at him. "I'm sorry about yesterday. I don't know what got into me."

Crockett sighed. "You're forgiven."

"I know you mean the best for Annette and Valentine. I shouldn't have gotten weird."

"Whatever. Thanks."

"Okay." Last perked up. "Brothers?"

"Brothers." They pounded each other on the back once, then Crockett headed off. He could understand what Last meant about being weird about Valentine. Even after sculpting her curves, Crockett was having a hard time forgetting about her.

"Uncle Crockett! Uncle Crockett!"

Kenny and Minnie ran over to him. "How's my best kids?"

They hugged him, and the tension he'd been feeling melted away.

"We're good. We want to go to town. Can you give us a ride?"

"Where's your father?" Crockett asked. He was being wooed for something for sure.

"Painting something," Minnie said. "We need to run an errand for Mom."

In the distance, he could see Olivia working Gypsy. Barley stood nearby, leaning against the post, every once in a while gesturing some instruction. Next to Barley was Mimi's father. Now that the sheriff was on the mend, Barley dragged him out to the ranch from time to time.

"Your mother doesn't have any idea you're trying to weasel a ride into town," Crockett said. "So what's up?"

"We want a cookie," Kenny said. "And we want to go to the hair salon. We heard that Ms. Lily adopted a stray."

Crockett sighed. Strays and cookies on a warm summer day. "I can play hooky for a bit," he said. "Load up."

"Yippee!" They ran off to tell Olivia

where they were going, and Crockett headed to his truck.

Actually, a cookie sounded good—if it was from Baked Valentines.

VALENTINE WAS SURPRISED when Crockett walked into the bakery with Kenny and Minnie. He was tall and handsome, and the kids loved him, and the whole scene—of a big cowboy corralling constantly moving kids—made her smile.

She loved living in Union Junction. She adored being part of the Jefferson family, even if it was an extended part.

"What's up, Crockett?" Valentine asked with a smile.

"They dragged me into town for a cookie." He leaned against a wall while the kids stared eagerly into the glass case. "You painted this place."

"I did." Valentine was pleased he'd noticed.

"I like the soft blue," he said, glancing around approvingly.

She smiled. Of course Crockett would

notice everything. He was supposedly a wonderful artist. "And I wallpapered the bathroom and back of the store with a pretty blueberry and lemon design. Very French kitchen."

"When do you find time for everything you do?"

Valentine smiled. "When Annette naps."

He looked at her, remembering how the brothers had doubted her at one time. It just went to show that anybody who wanted to make something of themselves could, if they were given a helping hand at the right time.

She certainly had made her mark on Union Junction.

Kenny and Minnie selected cookies, a frosted rose for Minnie and a powdered chocolate crinkle for Kenny.

"Thank you, Aunt Valentine," they said, scurrying across the street to the Union Junction beauty salon where Lily, her host of stylists and the new stray resided.

"That was sweet of you to bring them to town," Valentine said.

"I was shanghaied."

"Sure." She laughed. "Cookie?"

"Nah. I don't eat many sweets."

"Crockett! All you Jeffersons eat a ton of sweets!"

He grunted, looking around at the empty shop. Every white-painted table in the room seemed to have napkins and cups on it. "Break in the action?"

"Yes." She closed a cabinet and straightened. "If you'd been here five minutes ago, you would have seen half the town. I ran a sale for charity between eleven and twelve. All donations go to the pet adoption center Lily has decided to open."

"Good cause." He tossed some money into the jar he now saw on the counter. It was stuffed full of bills. "Nice haul."

Valentine beamed. "Everybody wants good homes for pets. Thankfully, Lily decided it was a project she could handle."

"Glad I missed the crowd."

"Come back and see the wallpaper."

He didn't care about wallpaper, but he willingly followed Valentine. "You did this yourself?" he asked, staring up at the scalloped edges neatly encircling the room. Sunny lemons and blueberries decorated the French vanilla-colored walls. "Cheery."

"Thank you. I'm very proud of it." Touching his arm, she said, "I want you to tell your brothers that I'm taking good care of their investment."

"Oh, hell, I don't think they care—Valentine, everybody's just happy that you're happy. You bring something special to the ranch, and we were glad to give you a start. I'm proud of you."

She smiled at him. "But I don't think you know what it means to be given a chance." How could she explain? Her destiny was in her own hands now; her talent was her future—because of their faith.

"I'd like a chance," Crockett said.

She looked at him. "At what?"

"I don't know. Maybe you."

"Oh." Was he saying what she thought he was? "I don't think so."

"Because it's a bad idea?"

"Yeah. A very bad idea. I'm sure of it." Valentine shook her head. "I don't want to ruin what I've got at Malfunction Junction."

"Okay."

Uneasy silence surrounded them. In her mind, Valentine knew she'd said the right thing, but what about her heart? "It's probably not a good idea to say this, but there *are* times I have thought about you."

He leaned closer to hear her soft voice as it trailed off. "I respect that you need your life to stay calm. You've been through a lot. My brother hasn't treated you as well as he should have."

Valentine held her breath. "He's not you."

Crockett seemed taken aback for a moment, then he only nodded and touched her cheek.

He wasn't going to do more, Valentine realized, and the fact that she had to make the first move gave her the strength to do it. There was no hurry, it was just the two of them in a quiet bakery. He watched her through dark, curious eyes and Valentine rose on her toes, lightly brushing her lips against his.

Then she waited, watching his expression. What would she see in his gaze?

He pulled away silently. Then he took the chocolate frosting spoon lying on the table and brushed it across her lips.

He licked her mouth clean, kissing her as she had never been kissed. Valentine's knees went weak, her blood thundered and tears sprang into her eyes. His touch felt so good! Nothing had ever felt so perfect.

She was surprised when Crockett stepped away from her. "I can't—" he said.

"What?" she asked softly.

"I shouldn't have done that," he said. "I may not be so different from my brother after all."

He walked out of the bakery. The tinkle of the bells on the door let her know he had gone. Valentine touched her lips in wonder. Maybe he regretted their kiss, but she certainly didn't. Crockett kissed like a dream.

Of course, he *had* frosted her. And what woman could resist being a lickable treat?

Her gaze fell on the pastry board across the room.

A new, exciting, almost *shameless* idea blossomed in her mind.

"WERE YOU EATING CAKE, Uncle Crockett? Did you bring us some?" Minnie asked as they sat in the truck.

Crockett frowned. He had been hungry for something, and it wasn't cake. "No. Why?"

"You have chocolate on your face," Kenny observed. "Right on your mouth."

Crockett cleared his throat. "I might have tried a little something sweet," he said.

"Valentine bakes real well, doesn't

she?" Minnie asked. "Dad says if Last was smart, he'd ask Valentine to marry him."

"What?" Crockett cleaned off his mouth with a handkerchief.

"I hope he doesn't," Kenny said. "I don't want Valentine to have to stay home and have more babies. I mean, I like Annette, but Valentine bakes my favorite things. Even Mom says it's worth a drive to town just to say hello to Valentine and see what she's got in the oven. We keep a special jar of change marked Valentine's."

Crockett was astonished by Calhoun's suggestion that Last should marry his one-night flame. It just showed how crazy Crockett had been to kiss Valentine. He had a funny feeling no one in his family would think him romancing the tempting little baker was a good thing.

"I don't even like chocolate," he said.

"Then why did you eat it?" Minnie asked curiously.

"Because it tempted me," he said. "But

I'm giving myself a deadline for getting over it."

"What's a deadline?" Kenny asked.

"It means doing something by a certain time."

And he planned to get Valentine off his mind by the time her Father's Day picnic rolled around. He had just about one month.

Chapter Five

"You have chocolate on your face," Mason said when Crockett walked into the house.

"Still?" Crockett took a look in the hallway mirror and rubbed at his face again, this time removing all traces of the kiss he and Valentine had shared. "That stuff has staying power."

"I wouldn't know. I haven't had time to sit around and eat bonbons lately."

"Shut up, Mason, you ol' sourpuss. You had your chance at frosting." That's when Crockett saw the note beside the phone. "Need cowboys for charity rodeo." He glanced up. "*Marvella* is giving to charity?"

Marvella was the owner of the Never

Lonely Cut-n-Gurls salon in the nearby town of Lonely Hearts Station, Texas. Over time, the Jefferson brothers' relationship with her had grown difficult. They were friends with her sister, Delilah, who owned a rival salon across the street from Marvella's. The two salons—and the two sisters—battled constantly, for customers, for stylists, for any imagined infraction. And Marvella had never been known for her charity.

Valentine had been working for Marvella when she'd first met Last. It had been Marvella's idea—and her threats—that had convinced Valentine to begin the paternity lawsuit against Last. Luckily, Valentine came to her senses before any damage was done, and she'd been more than happy to leave her work as a stylist at the Never Lonely Cut-n-Gurls salon for the world of baked goods.

"Yeah," Mason answered. "Delilah's got Marvella on a do-good kick, and it seems to be softening the old girl up. Gotta reinforce that when we can."

Crockett scowled. "Are you going?"

"Probably. It's good for us to do charity work. Besides, I haven't rodeo'd in a while."

He'd been too busy chasing the elusive Maverick and chewing off his brothers' heads. Crockett shrugged. "I guess I'm game if everybody else is."

"So…" Mason said, coming into the kitchen. "Speaking of Marvella, a little birdie told me you might be developing a soft spot for one of her ex-employees, Valentine."

"Not really," Crockett said, "but damn that birdie. What is the location of its nest so I can teach it not to idly gossip?"

Mason held up a hand. "Don't go off all hotheaded. It was purely speculation."

Since Jeffersons speculated on each other's business, it was hard to say "butt out." Crockett sighed. "I took Olivia's kids into town, and now I'm behind on my chores. See ya."

But before he could leave Mason looked at him funny. "You know, it would probably be a good thing if you went to visit Delilah, maybe stayed in Lonely Hearts Station for a few days."

"What the hell?" Crockett was totally annoyed. "Because of some little birdie?"

"No, because Last isn't sure how he feels about the whole thing."

"There is no *thing,*" Crockett said grimly. "If there were, you'd be the first to know, I'm sure, because Last would come telling tales to big brother. Besides, I don't know why a *thing* would be a problem since Last treats Valentine like leftover soup most of the time."

"That's between the two of them." Mason's tone was stern, and Crockett felt his blood hit slow boil.

"There is no *them.*"

"Rome wasn't built in a day."

"Yeah? So you're saying that, given time, there might be a *them?*" A tiny bit of guilt and a whole lot of jealousy crept up on Crockett. So he tried to change the subject. "There's been plenty of time for you and Mimi, but maybe some Romes never get built."

Mason frowned. "I signed you up to ride a bull for Delilah's salon, Blood-thirsty Black."

"What?" Crockett stared at his brother. As good as most of them were at rodeo, none of them had been able to stay on Delilah's beast, which had finally won his registration as a bounty bull. "Last whines to you about me so you register me for an ass kicking? Don't you think it's time you realize the baby of the family is all grown-up, Mason? You don't have to protect Last anymore. He's quite capable of handling himself."

Mason shook his head. "You've been at loose ends ever since you gave up paint-ing. Calhoun trying his hand at the old paint box shouldn't have bothered you the way it did. But sometimes brothers feel things deeply, and you've been in a funk ever since you gave up the thing you loved best."

"*I've* been in a funk?" Crockett felt

white heat creeping up the back of his skull. "What have you been in ever since Mimi married Brian?"

They stared at each other. For the first time, Crockett wondered if they might come to blows. Over the years, he'd battled with his twin, Navarro, but never with his big brother Mason. Mason usually commanded the utmost respect.

But not at this moment.

"She's divorced now, Mason. Free as a bird. And if you're wooing Mimi with this Rome-wasn't-built-in-a-day method, can I just tell you that's how you lost her in the first place?" Crockett took a deep, torn breath. "Time is not our friend, Mason."

Mason had turned as pale as the French vanilla paint in Valentine's kitchen. Crockett felt pretty certain his brother thought he was doing all the right things—but the fact was, Mason's "right" wasn't everybody else's "right."

"Don't lecture me about Valentine, Mason. I have my own definition of what's right and what's wrong. I'll ride

Delilah's bounty bull, but only because I want to help an old friend. Next time, how 'bout you hop *your* ass atop ol' Hooves Of Death? Frankly, I don't have a whole lot to prove. You sure as hell *might*."

He left the kitchen, his chest tight. Mason had no business lecturing him. And Last had no right to run telling tales to Mason.

Crockett stopped in his tracks, forcing himself to breathe deeply. The truth was, he *was* romancing Valentine, not a lot, but a little. And obviously there were hard feelings about it. Even he and Valentine both seemed to know that they were flirting with disaster. His feelings were not exactly shiny clean. The residue of guilt and the frequent jealousy told him that.

If it hadn't been for Last's wild night on the town, Valentine wouldn't be living on the ranch. And if she became uncomfortable with her friendship with Crockett, she might leave.

That was the last thing Crockett wanted. She had a good home here. Valentine was happy and grateful for her newfound independence. She was trying to please the brothers by making good on their investment. And Annette had people around who doted on her. Even Minnie and Kenny made special efforts to play with her and coddle her like a little sister. But if Mason felt the need to broach the subject, then matters had heated up.

What had Crockett been *thinking?* A sweet kiss was heaven, but he should have learned his lessons about forbidden fruit from watching his brothers in various stages of downfall. Brothers could unwittingly cause each other all kinds of pain.

Like the pain Calhoun had caused him by trying out painting. Like the pain good-hearted Mason caused everyone. Like the pain he had probably caused all his brothers at one time or another without ever knowing it.

If matters had become uncomfortable and someone needed to leave the ranch so that Rome could be built in some form or fashion…it would be Crockett.

Until that became necessary, he resolved to stay as far away from Valentine as was humanly possible.

ON THE DAY OF THE RODEO, Valentine watched Calhoun and Olivia fix a bridle for Minnie, smiling at how easily the couple worked together. Maybe one day she and Crockett would have that type of relationship, she thought wistfully.

The daydream surprised her. One small kiss and she was thinking of a life together? Most likely the kiss hadn't meant anything to him. He was probably doing what Jefferson men did with willing women—amusing himself. After all, the Jefferson brothers were not immune to women, and women loved those men because they were always rough and ready.

And she *had* made the first move.

"Valentine, is something wrong?" Olivia asked. "You seemed so happy a second ago."

"No. I'm fine." She gave Olivia a smile. "I've been thinking about a new recipe."

"Oh, I know all about the mood of creation," Olivia said. "When Calhoun is working on a project, he gets very quiet."

Valentine stood. "I should get to the bakery."

Calhoun looked surprised. "You're not going to the rodeo?"

"Oh, no." Valentine tucked a lock of hair behind her ear, patting Kenny on the head as she stood.

"We can give you a ride, of course," Olivia said.

"Come with us," Minnie said. "It's going to be fun. All the brothers are going to ride!"

"I'd better work," she murmured.

She didn't want to run into Marvella, and she didn't want to see her old coworkers from the Never Lonely Cut-n-Gurls salon. Once she'd left, those ties had forever been broken. It would be awkward, like a player who was now on an opposing team, despite the fact that Marvella and Delilah were said to be behaving just like sisters these days.

"Have fun." She smiled and excused herself, walking toward her truck. "Somebody call me and tell me how it went."

Just then Crockett pulled up in his truck. Valentine smiled and waved, slowing her steps a little so he could catch her and chat if he wanted to. He didn't. Glancing over her shoulder, she realized he'd gone right to his brother. When he looked up and saw her peeking his way, he gave a brief nod.

Valentine's heart sank. Maybe he was very busy and hadn't had a chance to be more outgoing.

But a moment later, when she heard Crockett's truck roar off into the distance, she knew their kiss yesterday had been a bad idea. And as for that shameless creativity he'd inspired in her that day? It was probably best to let all the bad ideas go.

"Who was I kidding?" she murmured. Of course the specter of Last had given him pause. It was so unfair, and the next time she saw Crockett, she was going to tell him so!

But looking up at the main house, she knew she would do no such thing. Her life here was good, and it was secure for her daughter. If, for whatever reason, Crockett had decided that he didn't want to spend time with her, then she would accept that and stay in her own corner of the ranch. Their friendship had always been easygoing and pleasurable. She didn't want to lose that—with him, nor with the Jefferson clan as a whole.

"Valentine!"

Raising her head, she saw Last heading toward her.

Chapter Six

Valentine waited for Last.

"Hey," he said. He had Annette trundling behind him in a little red wagon, which made Valentine smile.

"Hi," she said to Last. "Did you get a wagon?" she asked her broadly grinning daughter.

"I was thinking about taking her into Lonely Hearts Station with me," Last said. "Do you mind if she goes to the rodeo?"

Valentine was astonished. Last's fathering skills seemed to be improving by the day. It was as if he'd discovered fatherhood was the most fun a man could have.

"My brothers and I are riding. And

Helga's coming this time. She said she'd help keep an eye on Annette."

"I think she'd love it." Valentine found it hard to meet Last's eyes now that she'd kissed his brother. Not that Last had any reason to care, but still a little guilt nudged her conscience. "Wouldn't you love to go to a rodeo, Annette?"

Her daughter simply continued to grin. Valentine smiled, thinking how different her daughter's life might have been if Mason hadn't decided to make a home for them at the ranch. "Of course she should go," Valentine said.

"Do you want to come with us?" Last asked.

Startled, Valentine looked up to meet his gaze. He looked sort of hopeful, but not in a romantic way.

"I'm trying to put the past behind us," Last said.

"The past?"

"Yeah." He nodded. "I haven't been as nice to you as I should have been. I regret that, and I'm sorry. It's not a good excuse, but I needed to do some growing up."

"And then what?" Was he suggesting they become a whole family?

He shrugged. "And then hopefully we raise a happy child who understands that both her parents are good people."

That didn't sound like a flirtatious move. "Okay," she said. "I'm good with that." Whatever was best for her daughter, she was willing to try. "Thank you for the offer of a ride, but actually, I was planning on working today."

"But the rodeo's in town!"

Valentine laughed. "And you may recall that I once lived in Lonely Hearts Station. I have seen many a rodeo and many a Jefferson ride. Always a fascinating event guaranteed to bring in the customers. However, today I have festivities of my own."

She kissed her daughter and gave her a little hug, which Annette returned. "You enjoy watching your uncles. No doubt one of them will need a sweet baby kissie to soothe the ouchies they get from getting tossed."

She would miss her daughter today, but one thing she appreciated about the unusual relationship with Last was that they never fought over time with their daughter. Annette would love the rodeo, and Valentine had work to do.

"Don't get hurt," she said. "Ride safe, Last."

Nodding, he left, pulling Annette's wagon.

She hoped Crockett wasn't the one who got the ouchie, because she had a funny feeling he wouldn't come to her to get a kiss for it.

CROCKETT HAD SEEN Last wheeling the wagon down toward Valentine's truck, so, even though he knew he was stooping way too low, he parked his truck behind a barn and watched them as they stood together talking.

It was wrong. Since he had decided to stay away from Valentine, he shouldn't care. Still, the jealousy monster had kicked back in. Telling himself that a man with information was a smart man, he excused his spying and—again—watched his brother.

Was Last romancing Valentine? Did he want to mend his ways and make a family with her?

Crockett could certainly understand if he did. If Annette was his little girl, he would want her to have an intact family. Life wasn't always perfect—the brothers were a good example of a dysfunctional family—but Crockett would sure put the work into trying for perfect. Loving Valentine would be no hardship on a man. She was sweet. Talented. Dedicated, and a wonderful mother.

He watched as she bent down to kiss Annette—and then realization hit him painfully in the gut. This was not just mere attraction—it mattered to him that she be happy.

And if that meant she should be with

Last, then why was he standing here spying?

He got into his truck with a heavy heart and drove away.

AT HER BAKERY, Valentine once more read over the recipe she held in her hand. Since there was a rodeo in Lonely Hearts Station, most of Union Junction had headed that way, partly for the fun of the rodeo and the charity event, but mainly to see the Jefferson men ride. So Valentine had locked up the shop doors, and she now sat on a tall wooden stool in the back of her shop, pulled up to the very pastry table where Crockett had kissed her senseless.

She may have had to give up her daydreams about Crockett, but she didn't have to give up the exciting idea he'd sparked in her with that kiss.

She pulled out a piece of paper and a pencil. Carefully she drew the shape of a gingerbread man, only this one had legs that ended in the shape of boots. Instead of a completely round head, she drew one topped by a cowboy hat. The corners probably wouldn't bake as uniformly as rounded heads. She needed a mold.

Making one of those was best accomplished using thin tin strips that she could shape with needle-nose pliers. Here at the bakery, she didn't have any needle-nose pliers, but she knew where she could find some.

Minutes later, she let herself into the main ranch house. It seemed strange that the house was so empty. She'd never been here alone; usually at least Helga was on the premises. Without the men the house lacked vitality and spirit. Valentine stood very still in the hallway listening to the silence.

This was what her life would have been like without the Jefferson brothers.

She didn't like it.

Hurrying into the kitchen, she headed toward the toolbox under the sink but a clay figurine on the counter caught her eye. She stopped and picked it up. Long hair was drawn into the clay, but the face had been left blank. Her curves were womanly, and she had a lushly bountiful rump tattooed with a tiny heart. The initials CJ were carved into the heart in tiny letters.

Air caught in Valentine's chest. Crockett had obviously begun working with a new medium, and he clearly liked this nude well enough to carve his initials into her bottom.

Who was this woman?

She'd had no idea Crockett had a lady friend. Especially one he'd seen nude. She felt flattened, and near tears. So why had he kissed *her* then?

The answer to that was simple. He hadn't. She'd kissed him, and he'd responded. Then he'd left. Today he'd wanted nothing to do with her.

Now she understood. Tears stinging her eyes, she reached under the sink, grabbed the pliers and escaped.

TWO HOURS LATER, Valentine had herself back under control. Crockett wasn't the only person who needed a creative out-let. Her newest idea would be her most fun creation yet; a wonderful way to ease her pride and get her mind off Crockett.

She looked at the rows of gingerbread cowboys laid out in strict marching order. "It certainly doesn't hurt as much to think about impossible cowboys if you're going to bake them the way you want them," she told her "men" with a smile. "Not bad for a trial run."

Something was missing, though, and a moment later she was twisting two new molds, a boy and a girl. With some frost-ing and decoration, she would have cook-ies to give the children at Christmas.

With sure hands, she formed a skirt on the girl and a darling pair of pants on the boy cookie. Smiling, she cut out a candy cane and laid it atop their hands, joining the two cookie children.

"Perfect," she whispered, then took the candy cane off and mashed the dough to reroll it. She would save the candy cane for Christmas. She wanted these cookies for her belated Father's Day celebration, so she rolled a heart and used it to join the children's hands. On the gingerbread cowboys she put hats and holsters.

She didn't let herself watch the clock, although by now the rodeo had to be warming up. Annette would love that. Valentine made two small girls and put them together in a wagon-shaped cookie mold, for Nanette and Annette.

Valentine sank onto her stool, looking with pride and a critical eye at her work.

Again, she knew something was missing.

The cowboys were very studly in their hats and holsters, but she hadn't quite captured their spirit. "Heart," she whispered, which of course was what the Jeffersons were famous for. Hard grunt-work, loyalty, charm, generosity and *heart*.

She carved out twelve tiny hearts. Did she want frosting?

"No, not for you gentlemen," she said.

Instead she pressed colorful decorations into the dough for eyes and sparkly hat bands. The final flourish would be each man's name drawn on his cookie, personalized like the stockings that lined the Malfunction Junction stairwell at Christmas.

Hopefully this would be the perfect special touch for the Father's Day picnic, to celebrate the men who had made everything possible for her.

They need not ever know that after all their attempts to make her feel like one of them, she never could be. Her broken heart wouldn't allow it.

TWO HOURS LATER, Valentine had finished the baking. Pulling the gingerbread men from the oven, she smiled with satisfaction. Nice and thick, they were perfect for munching.

She decorated each costume differently, drew each cowboy's name on his or her body, and attached the hearts. Carefully, she put the rather large family in a basket lined with a white lace napkin. The brothers who wouldn't be attending the picnic would get eaten by everyone else, but she resolved to replicate her idea at Christmas and maybe even refine it.

Banging on the back door behind her made her jump, her heart pounding. Everybody she knew was in Lonely Hearts Station!

"Valentine! It's Crockett!"

Surprised, she opened the door. "What's wrong? Why aren't you at the rodeo?" she asked as he strode inside the back room.

"I've come to get you." He glanced at her basket. "I've looked everywhere for you. You've been here all the time?"

She thought about the nude woman she'd found at the main ranch house. "Yes, I've been here all the time. Absolutely. This is where my work is."

He looked at her as if he didn't believe her, but all he said was, "You need to come to the rodeo."

"Have you ridden already?"

"No." He shook his head. "The amusements are in the afternoon. Riding is at night. So come on. You haven't missed a thing. You can't work all the time."

"I really can't go." She remembered the kiss she'd asked for, right in this room, and she knew she was safer here, away from Crockett.

"I know what's bothering you," Crockett said.

"You do?" Valentine certainly hoped not. If he ever figured out *he* was what was bothering her, she would be so embarrassed.

"Yeah. But you know, you and Marvella have to work things out eventually. You can't avoid her forever." He took a deep breath. "I know she didn't treat you well. But I swear I think she's trying to change. I really believe her witchy soul might be trying to—are those freshly baked cookies?"

"Yes." Valentine drew back so he couldn't see that the cookies bore the names of the Jeffersons. She didn't want to spoil the surprise after all her planning!

"They smell fabulous. How about I

give you a ride to the rodeo, and you give me one of those cookies?"

His slow and sexy grin unnerved her, making her want to say yes. "No," she said stubbornly.

"Oh, come on, Valentine," he said teasingly, approaching her with every intention of grabbing the basket.

"No, Crockett," she said again, moving clockwise around the pastry table. "These are for someone else."

"Is it a shut-in?" he asked. "Someone old and feeble who needs cheering up?"

She moved farther as he continued his advance. "No."

"Then they'll have to share." Grabbing playfully for the basket, he almost got it. A cookie popped out and fell to the floor.

Valentine gasped. "Oh, no!" Kneeling down, she reached for the cookie, but Crockett picked it up first.

"I'm sorry, Valentine," he said, kneeling. "I shouldn't have been playing around. I was picking at you, thinking if I teased you, you might decide to come with me to the ro—*Crockett*," he read as he turned the cookie over and looked at it closely. Glancing up, he looked at her. "This has my name on it."

Distressed, she nodded. "I know."

He looked back down at the cookie. "I'm wearing a hat and a holster. For a cookie, I'm pretty cool looking."

"Yes. And you were wearing this. But now you're not." Valentine picked up the now-broken heart that had bounced off, handing two pieces to Crockett.

"Oh, that's not good," he said. "My heart is *broken*."

Chapter Seven

All the way down to his artistic soul, Crockett knew he had done a very bad thing by wrecking Valentine's creation.

Not to mention, he was a very superstitious guy.

He had known he shouldn't come looking for Valentine, not with everyone else at the rodeo. But he hadn't been able to stay away. Now look at what had happened.

"I can press a new one," Valentine said. "Or frost over it."

Standing, Crockett laid the cookie on the counter. Silently, he stared at it, then he laid the heart beside the cowboy. "I'm sorry," he said to Valentine. "Somehow I always do the wrong thing around you."

"It's fine. Really it is."

He shook his head. "We have this great nervousness in my family about broken body parts."

She moved it away from him so he couldn't ponder its broken condition. "It's a cookie."

"It's a representation of me."

"But this is baking, not voodoo. Relax." With water and something else—maybe liquid sugar—she reattached the pieces to the body. "See? Good as new."

He frowned. "I guess. I am a little mystified as to why a cookie has my name on it."

She gave him an arch look. "You'll have to stay mystified."

Well, he was. Valentine had many secrets, and if he didn't know better, he might take hope from the fact she'd personalized a cookie for him. Unfortunately, she had been holding a basket, and he suspected the basket contained a cookie for every Jefferson brother.

"I'm not the only person who's been working on a new creation," Valentine said.

"Oh?"

"I found a sculpture in your kitchen."

"I knew you'd been somewhere else today."

"A little clay woman. Nude, sporting only a tattoo."

Uh-oh. "I've been trying out a new medium."

"Very nicely, I'd say. You seem to know the woman intimately."

He hesitated. How could she not know it was her? Not that he'd ever seen her naked, but he'd certainly thought about it plenty. "I don't know her *intimately.*"

"Really? Except for the face, the detail was striking." She cocked her head at him, and he felt heat encircling his neck.

"I thought the face needed to be more or less blank," he said hurriedly. He wasn't about to admit that, because he'd seen her face, he had that committed to memory. It was the rest of her he thought about constantly. Plus he hadn't elaborated on the face because he didn't want his brothers ragging him to death about having a thing for Valentine. That would be misery for him.

This meeting hadn't gone well. He shouldn't have come. But it was just hard thinking about her being back in Union Junction when the rest of them were having fun, and he knew good and well she hadn't gone to the rodeo because of him and Last.

If he'd broken his cookie heart, though, perhaps tonight was his lucky night aboard Bloodthirsty Black! The family Curse of the Broken Body Parts seemed to occur only once—no one had ever been injured twice that he knew of. If he was falling in love with Valentine, then maybe he'd already taken his lumps in gingerbread form.

He considered that, taking in how pretty she looked in her apron, with a light dusting of flour on one cheek. Surely the rush of his blood every time he saw her was worth any pain? Where was the greatest source of pain—being near her and falling in love, or being away from her and denying himself the pleasure of looking at her and dreaming of her?

Valentine put his cookie into her basket and covered it with the pretty white napkin. "The recipe isn't perfect yet, anyway."

He thought right now was just about as perfect as it could ever be. What he needed was a kiss to top off his good luck.

"I don't think I can watch you ride," Valentine said. "I'd be too nervous."

That lifted his spirit. "Nothing to be nervous about. I only get broken in cookie form."

"At least it was something simple like your heart." She smiled at him. "If it had been your leg or your head, I couldn't have fixed it."

He stared at her. She had no understanding of how important his heart was to him. And he knew that kissing her without making her his would only make his heart hurt worse. "I'm going now," he said. "You coming or staying?"

Her big eyes widened. "It's very awkward."

"I'll smack Last if he says another thing."

She gasped. "I meant with Marvella and the stylists."

"Oh." He tried to look nonchalant and thought he might be failing. "I can't smack them. Not even Marvella. They're girls."

"And I wouldn't want you to smack your brother for me. I'm giving a Father's Day picnic for him. We've just gotten to a comfortable spot in our relationship."

Rats. There were times when he'd love to pound Last. "You know, when Last was a kid, we wouldn't have dreamed of smacking him. He was the baby, and we all protected him. The family compass, we called him." Crockett sighed.

"Maybe it's not a good idea for me to come with you," Valentine said softly. "I really feel like I might be the source of nonpositive change in your family."

"Actually, the changes happened before you came along." Crockett shrugged. "Hop in the truck. You never know. You might be the change we need."

"My work *is* all done, and I'd love to be at my daughter's first rodeo...."

"There. All agreed upon. Somebody will probably need bandaging up, and if you can do it with that water and liquid sugar trick, all the better."

"It doesn't work that way."

Grinning, he put his hat on. "We're big boys. We can take the pain. C'mon, little baker. We've got some road to travel."

VALENTINE LEFT THE cookies at the bakery, vowing to make Crockett a new one later when she returned—one that hadn't landed on the floor and had its heart broken.

Now, sitting in the stands across from the Never Lonely Cut-n-Gurls, her old co-workers and housemates, Valentine had to admit to feeling very uncomfortable. She had never sat on Delilah's side of the stands before, and though she was with her new family, she felt exposed. Her life had changed so much since she'd lived in Lonely Hearts Station. For the better, she knew.

Last loaded up in the gate and Annette watched her daddy in big-eyed wonder. Bad-Ass Blue burst into the arena a moment later and did his level best to rid himself of the cowboy without success. Last jumped off triumphantly, waving to the crowd.

Then he jumped up into the stands and gave his daughter a big kiss. "You brought me luck!"

Over her daughter's head, Last caught Valentine's eye. "And I'm sure you did, too."

She blinked, startled. "I doubt it. You didn't seem to need luck."

"Every cowboy needs luck."

Was he flirting? She didn't think so,

but… "Congratulations. You got a great score."

He didn't even glance at the judges. He just stared at her, his eyes questioning. "You're never going to like me, are you?"

Her heart stopped. *"Like* you?"

"Be friends. The way you are with my brothers."

She winced. "It's hard."

After a moment, he nodded. "I understand."

He left, and next to her, Mimi rolled her eyes. "Don't fall for that."

Valentine turned to her. "What do you mean?"

"The Jefferson men pursue when they want to and ignore when they want to. But they never, ever do something halfway."

"I really didn't understand what he was asking," Valentine admitted. "Is he talking friendship, or something else?"

Mimi sighed. "He is generally confused. Last's a pleaser. He wants everybody around him to be happy. That's great, but *you* don't want to be confused by it."

"So he's not—"

"No." Mimi shook her head. "A Jefferson male in hot pursuit is not easily mistaken. You'd *know*."

Valentine wasn't comforted. Crockett certainly hadn't been after her in hot pursuit.

"Be guilt free. I sense that he feels bad for the way he's handled things with you."

"Oh."

Mimi shrugged. "Then again, those boys are not always true to form. You do know about the Curse of the Broken Body Parts, don't you?"

"Crockett mentioned something about it."

Mimi's light brows rose. "Really? Well, then it's on his mind, isn't it?"

"What's on his mind?"

"The thing they all dread the most. The pain," Mimi said conspiratorially. "Crockett's loading up on Bloodthirsty Black, and no one has ridden that bull to the bell yet. Ever! So in just a minute, we'll all get to see if he's cursed. I have to say, as a close female friend of the family, I do enjoy watching them be afraid of *something*."

Valentine didn't want Crockett to get hurt. Her fingers squeezed together; she felt a nervous ache in the pit of her stomach. What if he really was injured?

The what-ifs were too awful to contemplate.

A second later, the gate shot open. Bloodthirsty lurched out, snorting and throwing hooves as if he had fire on his back and was determined to put it out. Crockett hung on, his head snapping, his body coiled with unbearable tension as he was flung back and forth. Valentine felt faint, but she squeezed Annette's hand to try to keep her daughter from being worried.

The buzzer sounded, and Crockett jumped to the ground. Clowns rushed the still-kicking bull toward the breezeway. The crowd was silent for a stunned moment, then they burst into a hurrah and applause and a standing ovation.

Crockett waved his hat to everyone, but when Valentine thought he might come over to get congratulations from his family and friends in the box, he turned and left through a small door instead.

Valentine felt her heart shrivel up inside her.

"That was strange," Mimi said. "He didn't even wave over here. He didn't look hurt to me. Did he seem hurt to you?"

"No, he wasn't even limping."

"Well." Mimi turned to look at Mason. "Your brother's got a stick up his backside. What's his problem?"

Mason shrugged. "I told him he had to ride the bounty bull because he'd been an ass to Last. Now he's won the high score. And the bounty prize money. He just became the big man at the rodeo, unless Last can ride the bull and score higher."

Valentine's breath caught inside her. "Why would Last ride?"

"It's just the way the challenge is done

here. Bounty bulls usually never get ridden to the buzzer, especially not that one," Mimi said. "I can't believe I just saw that. It was amazing."

"It's a stupid rule," Valentine said, standing. "I'm going to go tell Last not to get on that crazy bull."

Mimi turned. "Mason, you tell him. He'll take it better from you."

"That's a great idea," Valentine said. "Would you mind, Mason? Annette needs her father in one piece."

Mason and Mimi looked at her.

"What?" Valentine asked uncomfortably.

"You're awfully worried about Last," Mimi pointed out.

"Of course I am! It would upset Annette dreadfully to see her father hurt."

Mason nodded. "I'll tell Last to forfeit his ride. Although he may not listen."

IN A PEN TO THE SIDE of the breezeway, Last and Crockett were engaged in a heated battle. Valentine realized as soon as she

stepped around the corner with Mason—
Mimi had stayed in the stands with the
children—that there was more at stake
here than a winner's buckle.

"I don't think you should," Crockett said. "I think my spine is cracked, I
swear."

"You're in one piece. That's good
enough for me," Last said stubbornly. "If
you can do it, I can, too. And I plan on
doing it better."

Valentine gasped. "Last, maybe you
should listen to Crockett."

Turning, he glared. "Valentine, this
does not concern you."

She stepped back, stunned. "Your
daughter is in the stands."

"I'm going to ride."

Mason blew out a breath. "You're being
a jackass."

Last gestured at Crockett angrily. "If
it was anybody else in the family, you'd
be applauding their effort to grunt it out.
Fight through it," he mimicked Mason.
"Why is it different for me? It's a rodeo.

The rules are the rules. I want my chance to challenge the winner. It doesn't matter that he's my brother."

Crockett shook his head. "You shouldn't do this. You owe it to Valentine and Annette."

Last sprang, landing on Crockett, and they flailed on the floor. Rolling and punching, fists flying, they each scrabbled for victory.

"Mason! Stop them!" Valentine exclaimed.

Mason shook his head. "Give it a few more minutes. It's good for them to work some of this out of their systems."

Valentine felt ill. She had a funny feeling something more was going on between the brothers than a rodeo score; it felt uncomfortably as if they were fighting over her. But that was silly. Last didn't want her; he never had. They were fine with their relationship the way it was.

He was proving a point, Valentine realized. He was every bit as rough and tough as his brothers; he no longer wanted to be seen as the baby, though he was past that by many years. He was a man. He might have a child, which should prove his manliness well enough, but he wanted to prove his strength to his brothers, and to the people in the stands. And to himself.

Valentine realized it was a challenge he could not back away from, and the fact that Crockett had won the undisputed crown just egged him on. He saw Crockett as a competitor, both in the rodeo arena and outside it.

The men rolled by, sawdust and hay sticking to them.

They were silly! She'd had enough of them and their machismo. "I can't stand movie heroines who do nothing," she said apologetically to Mason. Picking up a bucket of water meant for the horses, she tossed the cold liquid over the grunting, struggling men.

They totally ignored the drenching.

"Not much fazes a man when he's got vengeance on the brain," Mason told her.

Then he reached down with big hands to separate the brothers. "That's enough," he said. "Last, if you're gonna ride, you'll need some juice in your battery."

Breathing heavily, the two brothers glared at each other. They actually looked to be in pretty good shape, Valentine decided. Clearly Mason knew what he was doing.

But none of this would have happened if Last felt more secure in his family, or if he'd developed a better relationship with his daughter.

The best thing was for her to slip away.

"Have it your way, Last," she heard Crockett say as she walked back to the stands. "It's your buckle to win."

"And I will," Last said.

"Or break something trying," Mason intoned.

"Yeah? Crockett didn't break anything. Don't ever say I should do something because of Annette and Valentine."

"I meant you shouldn't ride the bull because they were here, dumbass. You shouldn't scare them. You're too hot-headed these days. And I didn't break anything because I'm a good rider, not because I'm avoiding love."

So much for the family curse, Valentine observed as she hurried away. She didn't believe in silly superstitions—then she stopped in her tracks.

Not too long ago, Valentine and her sister, Nina, had gone to great lengths to keep their heirloom bed in the family. It was supposedly charmed with baby-making powers. Valentine believed in the charm. And that meant she was just as superstitious as Crockett and the rest of the Jeffersons.

"Nothing good can come of this," she muttered as she walked to where her friends and family were sitting.

"We're going to take a break for a while," she said, picking up Annette.

"Where are you going?" Mimi asked.

"We're going to take a tiny walk while D-A-D-D-Y antagonizes the great hairy B-U-L-L."

"Head over to my kitchen," Delilah Honeycutt, Marvella's sister, called from one row up. Her longtime trucker boyfriend, Jerry, sat next to her, nodding. "There are fresh strawberries on the counter, as well as some just-baked cookies. They won't be as good as yours, but they'll tide you over. Help yourself to the fridge, as well."

Valentine smiled. "Thank you so much."

"Borrow one of the rooms upstairs for an N-A-P," Delilah suggested, nodding at Annette.

"I appreciate that." It was a very generous offer, and Valentine was relieved. "Thank you, Delilah. See you all later."

She headed off. "You're a sweet baby," she whispered to Annette. "Your daddy is being a gorilla, but his brothers will get him out of his hair suit. Eventually. And what did you think about your Uncle Crockett riding that mean ol' bull?"

Annette didn't answer, but she stuck her fist in her mouth.

"I'll get one of Delilah's delicious cookies," she said, letting herself into the cool beauty salon. "There was a time when I didn't think I'd ever be inside this shop," she murmured. "I'm so glad times are changing."

The door opened behind her. "Hey," Crockett said, closing the door. "You bailing?"

Valentine nodded, happy in spite of herself to see him. "I kind of have to. You?"

"Nah. I've got to be brave. I'll either be mopping up a brother or giving him my buckle."

Valentine looked into his eyes. "Just give it to him."

He chuckled. "Last would not accept a victory that way." Rubbing a thumb along her chin, he asked, "Why are you so anxious to protect him?"

Chapter Eight

Valentine pulled away from Crockett's touch. "I'm looking out for him for the same reason you are."

Crockett doubted that, but he told himself his jealousy was ill-founded. "I suppose I should be happy that you care about my family."

She moved farther into the kitchen. "I'm surprised you care what I think. Did I just imagine the silent treatment you gave me this morning?"

Touchy. He couldn't blame her; there was confusion enough to go around. "I'm not trying to cross any lines that you—or anybody else—has drawn."

"This family could be a tic-tac-toe

board. There are no winning squares, just dividing lines."

"Ouch." He pulled off a dusty glove and sank into a kitchen chair.

She didn't turn around as she fussed with Annette's dress. "Are you hurt?"

"No, that was a mental pain. I hate to think of bad feelings between us. You are my niece's mother."

He watched for a shrug but he couldn't read her posture. She set Annette on the counter and washed the little girl's hands. He smiled at her conscientious mothering.

"What time is Last riding?"

"In thirty minutes. I should get back and loosen him up." Crockett sighed. "I came to apologize, Valentine, for that mess back there. You're right about the lines. I feel them, too. Although I may be uncomfortable, I shouldn't take it out on you or Last."

"Uncomfortable about?"

He shrugged. Could he be honest about exactly what he felt? Maybe at this point he wasn't certain what that was. "Part of me admires you. Admires you more than as a part of our family."

There. He'd admitted it. The words lingered in the air between them. His stomach tightened.

"Sometimes maybe I think of you as more, too," she said softly. She hesitated a moment before setting a teakettle on the burner. "Saying that doesn't make me feel any better, though. I really don't want to think of you in any way except as one more of the Jefferson men. So I try not to."

What had he expected her to say? Recklessly, he moved behind her, turning her to face him. He felt the warmth of the stove as it heated, sort of like his heart, which refused to grow cold. "I stayed on that bull because of you," he said. "None of my brothers have the reason I did." He ran his palms down her arms, enjoying the soft feel of her.

"What reason?"

Did he imagine that hitch in her breath?

Why not keep talking? Maybe her response would surprise him. "There's something about you that draws me in. I like thinking about you. And then I remember Last and I tell myself I can't think about you. I got up on that bull, and I told myself that for those eight seconds, I wouldn't think about you. I would think about saving my life. For eight seconds, I would be free."

She stared up at him, her eyes huge.

He shook his head as he stroked her cheek. "I was looking for freedom from the guilt, from the worry. From knowing it was wrong to see you in any way except as a sister. Only, the crazy thing was, as Bloodthirsty left the gate, all I thought of was you. You and Annette. And it was the shortest eight seconds of my life."

After a moment, Valentine pulled away slowly, leaving his arms cold. She didn't say a word, and he knew he'd said too much, felt too much.

So he left. And the pain in his heart

was far greater than the pain of a broken body.

And none of it could be fixed.

STUNNED, VALENTINE STARED at the floor as she listened to Crockett walk out the door. He'd shocked her into complete silence. The depth of his passion overwhelmed her.

Mimi had said a Jefferson in hot pursuit was unmistakable. Now she understood.

She also understood that what he spoke of could never be. Part of her wished the fantasy had not come alive between them, because now they could never go back.

She desperately wanted to make love with him. How wonderful would it be to give in, to spend time in his world—

Blinking her eyes against tears, she chose a teacup and put a fragrant tea bag into it. Bemused, she carried Annette upstairs and put her down for a nap. All the while her mind replayed the intense look on Crockett's face when he'd revealed his feelings to her.

"I'll make cookies," she murmured, remembering Delilah's offer to use the fridge. Baking, Valentine recognized, had become her comfort, her refuge in every storm. Taking a bowl of dough, she lifted the plastic wrap. Chocolate chip would make the house smell good, and she'd be helping Delilah…and she wouldn't think about what Crockett had told her.

Not even once.

From upstairs, she heard Annette call her. Probably worried about being in a new place, or perhaps she needed something to drink. Her mind preoccupied, Valentine set the bowl down next to the stove and hurried from the kitchen.

The plastic wrap flamed from the heat of the stove, setting a stack of old recipe cards on fire. Instantly, the seasoning rack above took the flames and the wooden kitchen cabinets began smoking.

The teakettle, fully warmed now, let off a shrill whistle. Valentine ran down the stairs, stopping in horror. "Oh, no!" she cried. "Oh, no!"

The whole kitchen now alight, Valentine ran upstairs, grabbed her baby and hurried down the back stairs toward the rodeo.

THREE HOURS LATER, Crockett was really, really worried about Valentine. She simply sat, staring at the rubble that had once been Delilah's kitchen and salon. Sensing her mother's mood, Annette sat in Valentine's lap, patting her mother's face every once in a while.

The town's volunteer fire squad had done their best to put out the blaze, but the odds of getting it tamed quickly had been slim. Delilah hadn't cried at the sight of her destroyed home. Instead she'd tried to comfort Valentine, to no avail.

But when Marvella, her sister, pulled Delilah into her arms, whispering how sorry she was, how sorry she was for everything, Delilah did break down.

Crockett saw Valentine's shoulders

droop. She was so dejected by what she had accidentally done. He wanted to hold her, but he knew he could not. She had not wanted to hear the words he'd told her when they were standing in Delilah's kitchen; he had felt her withdraw.

If he went to her now, he would feel more of that rejection. He could tell her heart was broken. There really was no comfort he could give her.

But there were blessings: everyone had been at the rodeo, so no one was hurt; Delilah said she was fully insured; the townspeople loved her, and the town fathers said they would help her rebuild, newer and better than before.

Also Jerry was there to comfort Delilah, his brawny arms folded as he stood nearby, watching the two sisters hug away the years of pain.

Yes, there were blessings, but he knew Valentine was too distraught to see any of those right now. He knew exactly what she was thinking: She'd burned down the kitchen of her old employer's one-time rival, and maybe no one would believe it had truly been an accident. Perhaps people would say that they'd always known she wasn't to be trusted.

Last must have understood some of the cares weighing on Valentine because he put Annette on his shoulders and helped Valentine to his truck.

Jealousy ripped through Crockett like a fireball. That was the move he could have made, had he not spoken too soon, revealing his heart and likely forever driving a wedge of discomfort between them. He looked at his smoke-stained clothes, brushing a hand against them before heading inside the rodeo arena to help with the teardown.

There really wasn't much else he could do.

He'd won the bounty, but he didn't feel much like a winner. In fact, he felt as if he'd lost something that mattered a whole hell of a lot to him, which he might not ever get back.

Chapter Nine

Numb and totally devastated, Valentine allowed Last to lead her away from the destruction she had created. She couldn't believe what she had done—poor Delilah!

This was no time to leave. If her heart was broken, Delilah's must be far more so. She owed it to Delilah to stay here in Lonely Hearts Station and do whatever she could to right what she had done.

"I can't go," she said to Last. "Thank you for trying to help me, but I need to stay here."

He looked surprised. Atop his shoulders, Annette picked at her daddy's cowboy hat. "Are you sure?"

"I'm positive. It's time I show a little bravery."

"Valentine, Delilah knows it was an accident."

That didn't make her feel much better. "I can't leave her here with nothing."

"She won't have nothing. If it wasn't for Delilah, Union Junction would have lost a lot more during the Great Storm. We won't let her or her employees go without." He frowned at her. "You need to rest. Staying here fretting isn't going to solve anything."

"But I have to stay," she said, knowing she was being stubborn and yet feeling certain she was doing the right thing. "Last, it's about showing that I care. I just can't walk away and leave my mess behind."

He stared at her, but she wasn't looking at him. Her gaze was caught by Crockett, across the street. She watched him hoist a bag of sawdust on strong shoulders, and carry it inside the arena.

Last sighed. "Valentine."

She turned her head. "Yes?"

"Are you staying because of Crockett?"

"No!" She glared at him. "Don't even get started with me right now."

"I saw him go over to Delilah's. I know you were there, too. Shortly after, he came out, and her kitchen caught on fire."

She gasped. "What are you suggesting?"

He shrugged. "There is nothing to suggest. It's just how it was. But it seems something's going on between you two, enough for an absentminded accident to occur. It's not like you to not pay attention."

"I think I flopped the dish towel too close to the burner," she said miserably.

"It's not like you," he repeated. "I think your mind was elsewhere."

"Lots of people let their mind wander. It shouldn't be a disaster."

"Maybe it's best if you take a break from all this."

"I don't need a break. I need to help." She knew how much it meant to possess her own home and business. She hated that she'd burned someone else's down.

"Okay. I might as well stay here, too. We'll need to move the ladies somewhere. They can't stay in those rooms above the salon. Although the firemen say the rest of the house is stable except for the kitchen, it sure does smell smoky."

Tears welled up in her eyes.

"Now, don't get upset," Last said hurriedly. "Maybe they can open some windows or something."

"Not for smoke," Valentine said miserably. "It has staying power."

"Come on. Let's not stand over here talking," Last said. "You know," he added with a grin, "I am mad at you."

"Why?"

"I don't get to ride Bloodthirsty Black now. You effectively ruined my chance to show up my brother by setting a fire. I think you did it on purpose."

That brought a tiny smile to her face. "I didn't, but I'm glad you're not riding. The whole thing is ridiculous."

He shook his head. "Rodeo is for real men."

She dabbed at her eyes with a tissue, smiling in spite of herself. "Real men know when to say no."

"Yeah, well. I never have. Come on, sweetie," he said to Annette. "Let's go see the horsies."

"Don't let her out of your sight," Valentine said.

"It's her mother who's dangerous," he said with a wink. "I just ride bulls."

"You're a jerk," she said, swiping at his arm. "I won't forgive you for that comment."

Last left, with Annette happily bobbing on his shoulders.

"You're in a better mood," Crockett said, walking up to her.

"I can't be in a better mood," Valentine said, wiping soot off his face. "But I do feel less like the earth is going to open up any second and swallow me because of my crime."

"Valentine, it was an accident."

"I take pride in my kitchen work. How can I set a kitchen on fire? Plus I feel terrible about poor Delilah. I burned down her kitchen and her business!" Tears sprang into her eyes again.

He nodded. She put her hands on her hips. "Why aren't you more upset?"

"Because it was an accident, and we Jeffersons have had plenty of our own." He stroked her hair away from her face.

She shook her head, not about to allow him to soothe her into thinking this was minor. "It was still stupid."

"Yeah."

She glanced up at him, surprised.

"Ladies get propositioned all the time and don't set houses on fire," he said, his tone teasing.

She sighed. "You're as bad as your brother. Did anybody ever tell you that you Jefferson males have situationally inappropriate humor?"

"A time or two. Hey, you want to help me move some things over to Marvella's for Delilah's stylists?"

She gasped. "Delilah's girls are going to go stay at Marvella's?"

"Yep. Delilah, too."

"What have I done?" she moaned.

"I think you brought two sisters together who needed a reason to get together." He pointed toward Delilah and Marvella. The sisters were busily loading a truck full of belongings so they could be carried across the street to Marvella's. "We offered them our house, and the Union Junction stylists have some room above their salon that they were eager to share, but the Lonely Hearts girls voted. They and Delilah say they'll stay with her sister."

"I can't believe it," Valentine said softly.

"It's a new day in Lonely Hearts Station," he said cheerfully. "Hope it's a good one. Come on. Looks like they've got the moving covered. I need to pick up another bag of sawdust."

She followed him, more because he seemed to be her lifeline at this point, rather than because she believed in her ability to be helpful.

"Hey," Crockett said as they walked inside the rodeo arena. "Don't worry so much. Delilah told me she'd been thinking about redecorating."

Valentine stared at the large, handsome cowboy. "Is that more inappropriate situational humor?"

He shook his head. "No. That's what she said. She came out of the rodeo, asked if you and the baby were out of the house and safe, then shrugged and said she needed to redecorate anyway."

"Crockett, how can I explain to you that the kitchen is the heart of the home? Having my own place means everything in the world to me. Destroying someone else's breaks my heart."

"I understand. You are a very bad girl. Perhaps I should spank you."

She stared at him. "You wouldn't dare, and I would be very annnoyed."

He grinned. "Anything to make you

quit feeling so guilty. It's a kitchen, and maybe a lot of smoke damage—"

"Crockett!" She glared at him.

"You are a prickly little thing."

"You don't have a serious bone in your body!"

"I do. I really admire your love of hearth and home. In fact, I hope I marry a woman who adores the kitchen as much as you do. It's what every man dreams of."

She crossed her arms.

"I would trust you in *my* kitchen."

The twinkle in his eye was irritating. "Had you not approached me in the kitchen, I would have been my usual calm and collected self."

"Ahh." He nodded. "So you're admitting that I get to you."

"Cockroaches would also cause me not to be my usual calm and collected self, Crockett. Don't get too proud."

He looked crestfallen. "That was uncalled for."

She laughed, knowing he was faking

his hurt feelings. "Well, you have succeeded. You made me laugh."

"That wasn't really my goal."

"Do you have goals, Crockett? You seem to live by your momentary impulses."

"I have goals. I had an important goal when I came to Delilah's kitchen. It was this." He pulled her close, kissing her deeply. Valentine thought she could feel her toes curling—yes, they were—and maybe even her hair. She had forgotten what a great kisser he was! *A girl would bake all day just to get some of this sugar,* she thought as he held her.

Then he set her away from him. "That was a momentary impulse," he said. "I do like to live by them."

She took a moment to collect her wits. "You taste like soot," she said, "but somehow, I liked it." Before she could focus on what had just happened she heard an odd sound. "What's that?"

"Sounds like a bull. They're all in their pens."

She turned to look at him. "So, was Bloodthirsty your last ride?"

He grinned. "A cowboy never says that."

"Superstition?"

"Fact. We don't want to get old. We want the thrill. We want the admiration of women. You wouldn't say you'd baked your last cookie, would you?"

"I hope I never do."

"Same thing. Although I am not as young as I used to be, that *may* have been my last ride. I seem to have felt it more than I should have." He came to stand beside her at the rail.

Even sooty and sweaty, she had to admit that Crockett was the most handsome man she'd ever seen. "I should be getting back to help," she murmured. "Thank you for making me feel better."

"So what happens after today?" he asked.

"What do you mean?"

He shrugged, looking out over the

empty arena. "I worry that I've crossed a line, and now you'll avoid me."

"If I can handle life with your brother, as awkward as we've made our situation, I think I can handle a little flattery from you."

"So kiss me again."

She laughed. "Don't push your luck, cowboy."

He sighed. "We could be the best of friends, given our situation."

"Not that good."

"Yeah. I guess if I really kissed you, you'd probably figure out a way to destroy this arena," he said ruefully. "Although I don't see a stove."

"Okay, there's a reason you're needling me," Valentine said, "so I'm going to indulge you. What effect are you going for? Anger? Rage?"

"Just good ol'-fashioned lust, I swear," he said. "Garden variety, can't-stop-thinking-about-your-mouth lust."

And darn him, if he didn't *really* kiss her. Every fiber of her body told her it was a bad idea. Everything between them was a bad idea, but he simply felt so good. He made her feel that everything was better in his world, his world was an awesome place to be. She sighed, leaning into him, winding her fingers into the shaggy hair coiling out from underneath his hat. The only thing on her mind was nothing but the feel of Crockett.

LAST DUMPED THE last bag of sawdust on the ground inside the arena, then stood, brushing off his hands. He could work cleanup crew at Delilah's, he could lay down fresh sawdust on the floor in the arena, he could help the ladies move their belongings to Marvella's, but there was something else on his mind.

He glanced down at his little girl. Annette stared up at him, her eyes big in her face, watching her daddy work. Of all the emotions he'd ever had in his life, the feeling of looking big in his baby's eyes was the best. Annette adored him without hesitation, without emotional baggage. In her world, he was her man, and every-thing he did was special.

He loved the daddy thing.

"You're pretty cute for a bug-eyed spud," he told her. She nodded her head solemnly, then sat down on the bag of sawdust and began playing with her dolly. "I don't know exactly when you grew on me. But you sure did."

Kneeling down, he looked at his pretty little daughter. She gave him a smile, then went back to messing with her dol-ly's hair. He couldn't remember loving anybody the way he loved this child. His brothers had taken care of him, and they had loved him, but Annette was his to care for, and somehow that was more spe-cial than anything he'd ever known.

He felt a moment's twinge of guilt that she would never know what it felt like to be part of a whole family. He'd cer-tainly known that loneliness. It was not good. What would he say to her when she grew up? *Mommy and I really never liked each other, so we didn't get married, even though we made you.*

That sounded terrible. Looking down at his daughter's soft hair, he tried again. *Mommy and I never liked each other, but we both adored you.*

It was going to be difficult when the questions came.

A remote part of him wondered if it would simply be easier for Annette if he and Valentine married. People had arranged marriages all the time! It would certainly change Annette's life for the better. Nobody asking uncomfortable questions at school, like why aren't your mother and father married? No teasing.

He would love to save her that pain. To do that, he and Valentine would have to agree that a whole was better than two halves. She wasn't likely to feel that way, he'd seen the way she looked at Crockett.

Some resentment bubbled up inside him. His brothers had no idea how hard it was being the baby. They'd congratulated themselves for years that they were such good parents, and they had been, but...there was a low-man-on-the-totem-pole effect to being youngest.

It wasn't as wonderful as they thought it was. He was forever fighting for his place, his share of whatever was happening. All the brothers looked up to Mason and were even slightly in awe of his temper.

No one was in awe of Last.

It stunk.

"I could have ridden that stupid bull," he told his daughter. "I could have beaten Crockett's score, if I'd had the chance."

It probably mattered very little to anyone except him, but matter to him it did. He always got the butt end of every situation in the family. Oh, hell, if the boot had been on the other foot, and Crockett hadn't gotten to ride the final ride with a chance to beat Last, all heck would have broken loose in the arena. Crockett wouldn't have let anybody beat him. He was still pouting over the fact that Calhoun had sold paintings before he had.

"I *could* have ridden that bull," Last repeated, and Annette looked up at him, her chubby, pretty little face angelic and adoring. She saw her daddy as a hero, Last realized.

It should be enough.

"It *will* be enough," he promised his daughter, "once I've ridden that bull. It's a man thing, and I'm just as vulnerable to that as any other red-blooded cowboy."

And once he rode that bull into a piece of leather fit for shoes, he would talk to Valentine about their nuclear family unit. Heck, they weren't in love, no way. But maybe she saw their lives the same way he did, with everything revolving around Annette and what was best for her. If Valentine said no, that would be fine.

But he was going to ask. For his daughter's sake.

Thinking he heard voices, he walked out into the breezeway. His chest tight, he watched Crockett kiss Valentine as if he was thirsty and had just found a watering hole.

Last jumped back into the shadows, glancing down at his child. She had followed him and stood staring up at him. "I have really made a mess of this," he told her, "and I'm not really sure how to fix any of it."

She held her dolly up to him with a smile. "Thank you," he said. "I don't believe I've ever had a doll before. If I did, it was probably your Aunt Mimi's. Although if she ever had one, she probably pulled its head off and gave it to Mason."

Annette took her dolly back from him, satisfied that he'd paid proper attention to it. "I've got a crazy idea," he said.

She looked at him curiously.

"Around this corner is Uncle Crockett and your mommy," he said. "Walk over to your mommy, okay?"

She nodded. When Valentine and Crockett broke away from each other, startled by Annette's presence, Last came around the corner, waving at them innocently. "Brought the last bag of sawdust," he called, as if he hadn't seen a thing.

"Thanks," Crockett said. Valentine smiled self-consciously. Last pretended not to see. He made sure Annette was securely in her mother's arms and then he left.

He and Mr. Bloodthirsty Black had some wrangling to do. And when it was over, one of them was going to have a different kind of reputation.

Chapter Ten

"This must be awkward for you," Crockett said. "I'm sorry."

Valentine looked up at him. "It's not awkward because of Last. I mean, it is difficult, but that's because of you. Not him."

Crockett frowned. "How do you mean?"

Valentine snuggled her daughter to her. "I feel things for you I shouldn't."

"How do you know you shouldn't?"

"I just have this funny feeling." She couldn't meet his eyes.

"A funny feeling because of Last."

"Yes. No. I don't think so. I just worry about what your brothers might think… so when I think of you, when you kiss me, I get all kinds of butterflies chasing around inside. The thing that worries me is that I don't think the butterflies are chasing because they're happy—it feels like they're nervous."

"Well, hey, I'm nervous all the time." Crockett smiled and touched a finger to Annette's nose. "You're probably nervous, too, aren't you?"

Annette stared at him, which made Valentine laugh.

"She is not nervous, she's content. This is a happy baby," Valentine said, squeezing her daughter. She drew strength from the sumptuous feeling of her daughter's petite roundness and warmth. "She is the reason I bake."

"Really? I was hoping it was me, when I saw that gingerbread cowboy."

Valentine shook her head as she nuzzled Annette. "I bake for her sake." Crockett didn't need to know that he was on her mind all the time. That knowledge would do nothing good for that double-layered confidence he possessed.

But she knew he'd figured out what she

hadn't said when he put a gentle, yet firm finger under her chin so she'd have to look at him.

"Valentine, I'd be very good to—"

The sound of a crashing gate jerked both of them around. To her horror, Valentine saw a bull leap into the empty arena. It was Bloodthirsty Black, and on his back was her daughter's father.

"Damn it!" she heard Crockett say. Before she even realized what was happening, before she even understood that Last had been flung from the bounty bull's back, Crockett had hurdled the rail, run into the arena, and began flopping his hat wildly at the bull.

Bloodthirsty was living up to his name, determined to wreak vengeance on the cowboy who had dared straddle his back. Last was down, Bloodthirsty was throwing dangerous hooves and Annette was screaming.

Or maybe it was her.

Crockett was down, too, thrown to the sawdust like a spoon thrown to the floor by a baby. Now more brothers rushed into the ring.

It was all over in an instant. She couldn't see what had happened, or how badly anyone was hurt, but Annette was crying. Valentine knew that the best thing she could do was take Annette out of the arena. Her tears would only make matters worse.

Valentine realized she was shaking as she hurried away. "It's okay," she told her daughter. "Don't cry, sweetie. It was just a game, and your daddy is fine."

Annette hiccupped. Valentine wiped at her daughter's eyes, then debated what to do. Outside, the specter of Delilah's burned kitchen greeted her eyes. Last and Crockett were hurt, and she had no idea how badly. She felt eerily as if everything was all her fault. An ambulance wailed, startling her from her indecision.

She wanted Annette gone before the medics carried Last or Crockett from the building. "I think we'd better go home," she told Annette. "You'll calm down…

and I think my presence has wreaked enough havoc."

Just then Mimi came out a door beside her, her long hair askew.

"Are they all right?" Valentine asked anxiously.

"I can't tell, actually. I do know it's more pain than either of them bargained for in their quest to avoid all things superstitious. Valentine, do you mind taking Nanette home? Helga can keep an eye on her, but—"

"I'd be happy to. Annette is upset because she saw—"

"I know. Try not to worry." Mimi handed her the keys to her truck. "Drive safely. I'll call you as soon as I can."

Valentine looked into Mimi's sympathetic eyes. "Thank you."

"Thank *you*."

Valentine strapped both the children safely into the double cab, took a deep breath to steady herself and drove out of Lonely Hearts Station.

As if she were running away from more than the man who needed her.

CROCKETT STARED AT Last with deep annoyance. They shared a room, their hospital beds next to each other. As hard as it was to get a glare going with his leg in a cast, Crockett craned his neck to be certain Last got an eyeful of his displeasure.

His frown softened as he looked at his kid brother. Knocked out from painkillers or whatever dope they had in his IV—or maybe just mercilessly out of his head from pain—Last looked like the kid they'd all protected growing up. The lines were smoothed from his face, though soot smudged his cheek, sawdust was in his hair, and there was a gash across his forehead from one of Bloodthirsty's hooves.

Crockett lay back against his pillow, unable to stay angry with Last. It had been a close call, but as bad as it was, it could have been so much worse.

He understood exactly what had driven

Last to try to ride that damn bull. Pride. Stubborn, heart-eating pride.

They all had a strong share of it.

And a lot of this was his fault, Crockett knew. He couldn't get away from the responsibility of knowing that Last was struggling with internal demons, one of which was his guilt about Valentine. What man wouldn't feel guilty about getting a woman pregnant and not loving her—not wanting to marry her—and yet not wanting anyone else to have a place in his child's heart.

I've really screwed this up.

"If I'd been smart, I would have left her alone," Crockett muttered to himself.

But he hadn't been, and now both he and his brother were busted up. With no true love or Curse of the Broken Body Parts to blame it on, either.

"Crockett?"

"Yeah?" Crockett rolled as best he could to peer at Last.

"I feel like crap."

He had a black eye, Crockett realized. "Hey, you look like crap."

Last smirked, or tried to, except he had some stitches around his lip and really couldn't. "Dude, that damn bull tore a chunk out of my hide."

"Tell me about it."

"You shouldn't have come in the ring," Last said slowly. "I didn't mean for you to get hurt."

"What, and leave my baby brother to get pulped? Nothing would have stopped me."

Last sighed. "I don't want to be the baby anymore. I think I should take my rightful place among the old farts in the family."

Crockett lay back against the pillow. "Trust me, it's not that happy a place to be. Old and lonely. So what?"

"Who's old and lonely?"

"Mason. You want to turn out like him?" Crockett asked. "And me. Right now, I've got a lonely broken leg. You've at least got a daughter, Last."

"Yeah."

Crockett heard the slight smile in his brother's voice. "All right, then. So quit wheezing about not wanting to be the baby. Your place in the family is a good one. Some of us would rather be Last than who we are."

Last sighed. "Where is Valentine?"

"She went home. Annette was upset when she saw the bull tossing you like she throws her toys."

"Man, I am such a screwup. What was I thinking?"

"None of us ever know what we're thinking right before we make some catastrophic, life-changing mistake," Crockett said. "Though I will say you've had more than your fair share of questionable moments." Crockett wiggled as best he could. "I want to scratch real bad, and I can't get to my leg. Share your IV with me."

"I would if I could." Last sighed. "Crockett?"

Crockett glanced over at him. His brother sounded tired.

"Hell, yes. Whatever it is you want, the answer is yes. I'm getting cranky with this itch and realizing how much I'm not going to be able to do in a cast. Shoot, I'm going to be out of work for at least two months, I bet. *You* sure as heck have rehabilitation in front of you. That leaves Mason to do everything. He's gonna lose his mind." Crockett rolled his head to look at his brother. "So what is it?"

"Don't take my baby away from me," Last murmured. "I'd give you my IV, my shirt off my back, anything I have. But don't take my baby."

Crockett's heart skipped. "What… about Valentine? Can I have her?" he whispered.

Except for a groan that could have been yes or no, there was no answer. Last had fallen asleep, rocked again into slumber by the medicine.

THE NEXT DAY, Mimi walked into Baked Valentines. Valentine looked up from her work with a smile. The little girls sat at

Valentine's feet, each happily banging spoons against muffin pans and enjoying the noise they were generating.

"Hi," Mimi said. "Concert?"

"We have a couple of budding composers." Valentine smiled. "Tea? Cookies?"

"I'd love both." Mimi pulled a stool close to Valentine's workspace, sitting down as she studied her. "How are you doing?"

"Oh, for a girl who burned down a kitchen and got a couple of cowboys stomped, I'm just fine."

Mimi laughed. "You have had some trouble lately. But it's not as bad as you think it is."

"Oh?" Valentine set a doily-covered plate in front of Mimi. "It sure feels like I am the conduit of all things miserable."

"You must be in love. Only people in love speak with such dark, doomed emotion."

Valentine smiled. "I'm not in love, but you are cheering me up."

"If you're not in love, do you think you

might be in strong like?" Mimi took a sip of the tea Valentine put in front of her and sighed with pleasure. "This is lovely. What is it?"

"Cherry peach. I'm also brewing up some blackberry lemon."

"Where do you get these wonderful teas? Some days I want to stop in just to see what you've got in the teapot."

"Fancy tea catalogues. Tea is so relaxing that I feel I should have as many different varieties as possible."

"I'll say. So, you're in strong like?"

Valentine nodded. "I've got a sinking feeling I am. It's sort of like being on a teeter-totter and knowing my partner is going to get off while I'm up high."

Mimi laughed. "Crockett wouldn't do that to you."

"At the rate I'm going, I'd probably do it to myself. I have turned into a walking disaster."

"That's all behind you now. And you'd be surprised at how many good things are coming out of your disasters."

"Like what?"

"Like…Delilah has decided to move her salon to Union Junction."

"Really? What about the Union Junction stylists?"

"They're delighted. It will be just like it was in the beginning, before Delilah had to let half of them go. Besides, they're wanting to get busy with their pet rescue project, so having extra hands will be awesome."

Valentine wasn't convinced. "Thank you for trying to make me feel better about setting Delilah's kitchen on fire, but it is hard not to be really embarrassed. I'm a baker, for heaven's sake. How can I burn down the place I love most in a home?"

"If the kitchen is the room you like best then you haven't been to bed with a Jefferson—"

Valentine blushed.

Mimi sipped her tea, then said, "Well, you aren't the only one who has awkward moments, as you can see. I'm sorry, Valentine."

"It's fine." Valentine smiled. "Mimi, do you have something to ask me?"

"No. I was simply saying that Crockett could probably change your mind about your favorite room." Mimi sighed. "I don't know why, but I never think of you with Last. I always picture you with Crockett. Isn't that odd? My mind just conjures the two of you together. It's as if you two and Annette should be a family. Come here, butter cake," she said, picking Nanette up.

Miffed at being disturbed from playing with her friend, Nanette let out a howl. "Back you go," she told Nanette. "Bang away."

Valentine sat down on a stool opposite Mimi and began rolling out dough. She didn't want to touch the comment about Crockett so she said, "They play so well together."

"I know." Mimi turned away from her daughter and back to Valentine. "I almost forgot. The other good thing that has happened is that Marvella offered to buy Delilah out."

A bad feeling hit Valentine. "How is that good?"

"She's going to rebuild and refurbish and open the building up as a shelter for women in need. With a bakery on one side and a few shops on the other. That way, tourists will be more tempted to come to town, and any women who stay there will have gainful employment. It's pretty much what Delilah was doing all along with her salon, only now it will be on a major scale. The town fathers are quite delighted, as is Delilah. She's thrilled that Marvella has changed, and that their relationship is on the mend."

"I'm glad," Valentine murmured. The Jeffersons would be happy to know their enemy had turned over a new leaf. And speaking of brothers… "When do the boys get out of the hospital?"

"Crockett sooner than Last. Last is under observation for a concussion and some other things. Crockett only has a broken leg, and it turns out he's the worst patient of the two."

"Really? I wouldn't have guessed that."

"Neither would Mason. Now that all the brothers, except for Calhoun, have left the ranch with their families, it's pretty much up to Mason to care for those two. And believe me, it isn't pretty." She laughed.

"I feel as though I should be doing something to help!"

Mimi shook her head. "This is not the time. Trust me. It's good bonding for them, don't worry."

Valentine pressed molds into the dough, thinking about Crockett and Last and all the complications between the three of them. "Have you ever known that something wasn't going to work out, no matter how appealing it might be?"

"You mean Crockett."

Valentine winced. Was she that obvious? "I mean, any relationship. I'm speaking in generalities."

"Sure." Mimi shrugged. "I have some

passing acquaintance with relationships that don't work out."

"Well, that's what it is with…a certain man and me," Valentine admitted. "Even if I allow myself to fantasize about him, I can never see a way it would work out so that everyone is happy."

"Maybe no one needs to be happy except you and…this man."

Valentine raised a brow. "And what about the budding maestra on the floor? She needs to be happy. I have to consider her feelings, too. One day she's going to be old enough to ask questions."

"Personally, I dread that day," Mimi admitted. "I've got some answers to give myself." She brightened. "Although my childhood was full of question marks, and I turned out fine. Maybe I'm worried about nothing."

"I like to consider every angle," Valentine said. "I'm kind of cautious like that."

"Women are naturally more cautious. Most men like to dive right into everything. We do a lot more soul-searching."

"Oh, dear," Valentine said. "One angle I hadn't considered. I'm planning a Father's Day picnic-party for Last—for all the fathers—and it's in a few weeks. I wonder if he'll be in any shape to enjoy it."

"Now that I don't know."

"Mimi," Valentine asked slowly, thinking of Brian's absence from the father's picnic, "not that it's any of my business, but…do you think Nanette will wonder why her father never comes to see her?"

Mimi cocked her head as she looked at Nanette, who she was holding. "As I said, I have a lot of answers to give when she starts asking. I'm hoping she won't ask for a long time."

Maybe she wouldn't. And maybe Annette would never care that there was no father figure in her home. She might be satisfied knowing there were bunches of men around who loved her. *I have a wonderful life: baby, bakery, everything,* Valentine thought. *There is nothing missing in my life.*

Except a father figure for Annette. And in a blinding moment of clarity, she realized she wanted a real, whole family for her daughter. Unlike what she and Nina had known growing up; unlike the way Mimi remembered her childhood. Valentine wanted a complete family for Annette.

The phone rang, and since Valentine's fingers were doughy, Mimi answered it. "It's Crockett."

"Oh. What does he want?"

"Crockett, Valentine wants to know what you want," Mimi said. She listened and then glanced at Valentine.

"He wants you to marry him," Mimi said.

Chapter Eleven

"I'm not sure how to take that," Valentine said.

Mimi laughed and shook her head. "I think he's got medicine head."

That sounded reasonable. Her heart, which had begun beating frantically, slowed to a regular pace.

Mimi cupped her hand over the mouthpiece. "The only brother that I can think of who proposed when he was out of his head was Ranger."

"But they're always a little out of their minds, aren't they?" Valentine asked.

Mimi nodded. "Crockett's speech is slurred, though. This is a different type of out of his mind."

Pharmaceutically induced or not, Valentine didn't like it. She'd already been propositioned by Last when he was under the influence, and she wasn't about to fall for that again. "Tell him no thanks."

"Valentine says no, thanks, Crockett," Mimi said, looking pleased to deliver the news. "He wants to know why not, Valentine."

"Because he's proposing unromantically, while he's lying next to his brother, over the phone." She mangled the cookie she was pressing and started over, rolling the dough.

"Last's asleep," Mimi said. "But Last told Crockett it was okay to ask you."

Valentine got up, snatching the phone from Mimi. "You did not ask Last if you could marry me!"

"Ish okay," Crockett said tiredly.

"Oh." Valentine's anger disintegrated. He sounded terrible! "Are you all right?"

"Think so. Going to sleep now."

The phone clicked off. Valentine stared at Mimi. "He sounds dreadful."

"I'll tell you a little secret—Jefferson men make the worst patients on the planet. Simply the worst." Mimi giggled.

"But I feel sorry for him."

"Don't. They have half of Lonely Hearts Station checking on them—trust me."

"All female, probably."

"Yes," Mimi said, "and the hot doctor that they're all crazy for is taking care of them."

Valentine had never considered that every single Lonely Hearts salon stylist and Never Lonely Cut-n-Gurl would be streaming in and out of Crockett and Last's room. "Drat!" she said, rolling another poorly shaped cookie. "My mind is just not on this today. I'd better make chocolate chip cookies instead."

"Mmm. My favorite," Mimi said. "I'll grease the pans since the kids are enjoying themselves."

"Mimi," Valentine said, taking a bowl from the fridge, "don't you think it was odd that Crockett asked me to marry him?"

"Oh, not odd. Very Jefferson. When they get something in their mind, it lodges pretty firmly."

Valentine set the bowl on the counter. "So you're saying, even if his proposal happened because he's out of his mind on medication, he really *does* want to marry me?"

"Yes. I think he likes you a lot. He's probably trying the notion on. Whether he asks once he's sober, I don't know." Mimi glanced at her. "Why? Would you like that?"

"I don't know," Valentine said softly.

"Well, there you have it," Mimi said with a grin. "Yet another Jefferson male in a conundrum. And he's hurt, which he'll probably consider a positive sign, Curse of the Broken Body Parts and all."

"But Last is hurt, too."

Mimi frowned. "That must be why Crockett asked you to marry him! He's competing to be the first one to ask!"

Valentine stared. "Because Crockett's

not certain which of them has got the actual Curse?"

"Exactly." Mimi brightened. "Competition is a good thing."

"Not to me. It means he doesn't really know if he cares about me. He just wants to beat his brother. That's how Last got hurt, trying to best his brothers."

"Don't mistake me, the Jefferson brothers would give each other a hand and their last dollar. But competing is the way they show affection."

"Well, I don't like it. I want to be loved, not competed for like a trophy."

Single motherhood had made her very serious, Valentine realized. Once upon a time, she might have enjoyed two men fighting for her, a lighthearted flirtation, a casual relationship. But the stakes in her life were higher now. She had a child. She had a business to run, which required careful planning. There was no room for her to be flighty.

For her sake, and especially for Annette's sake, any man Valentine loved had to be sincere. Dedicated. The Jefferson males were sincere and dedicated in some things, but when it came to matters of the heart, they could be *very* elusive.

The phone rang again, but this time Valentine answered. "Hello?"

"Valentine? I've been thinking—"

"So have I," she said. "Crockett, I wouldn't marry you if you were the *last* man in Union Junction."

SHE'D HUNG UP ON HIM. Last stared at the phone, then glanced over at his sleeping brother. So Crockett had proposed to Valentine, had he?

And she was obviously turning him down flat.

Very tough on a man's ego. Last grinned, feeling better than he had since he'd gotten stomped by Bloodthirsty. He couldn't remember ever hearing about any of his brothers being rejected, particularly not by a woman.

The Jeffersons always did the rejecting. He laughed, feeling better by the moment. Suddenly, he didn't feel like the one who could never live up to the standards set for him. Knowing one of his brothers had crashed and burned was a fine verification that they did not always win.

Then he sobered, even as the wonderful feeling of validation stayed with him. He glanced over at his brother curiously. Crockett lay in the bed, his leg raised, his face drawn and craggy as he slept. He looked terribly tired. In fact, even asleep, he seemed depressed, Last decided as he squinted at his brother.

He loved his brother dearly, and though he was happy to be a witness to Crockett's rejection, Last *did* want him to be happy. The fact was, this man had run into a ring to protect him from his own bad decision, a choice born of pride and stubbornness.

In his heart, Last wanted all his brothers to be happy. He always had. All their lives, he'd tried to be the one who kept the family together. God, he'd wanted them to be normal after their mother had died and Maverick had left.

"Damn it," he muttered. There was no Santa Claus, no tooth fairy, and no pot of gold under a Texas rainbow. It was just his brothers, and hard work, and in the end, love and compassion for each other.

Last wanted Crockett to be happy. And it appeared that Valentine made Crockett happy, or at least she did at this point in time. Mason used to say that the brothers wanted Molly on Monday, Trixie on Tuesday, Willow on Wednesday…blah, blah, blah. But he'd been right. At least until recently, the size of their commitment to females could fit between a mouse's ears.

Why Valentine would make Crockett happy, Last couldn't really understand. She was a wonderful mother and baker, but other than that the woman was a veritable tornado of disaster, an epic saga of her own making.

He could honestly say he was not in love with her. He loved her like a sister, like he loved Mimi, but he knew now that wasn't enough for either of them.

Frowning, he wished he could remember their night together. The male chauvinist in him wanted to say that a hellacious night of pleasure had resulted in his daughter, but it was strangely more like in vitro fertilization. He simply couldn't remember. They were tied together by their child, not by memories.

"I'm sure I was a stallion in bed," he told his sleeping brother.

Oh, hell, what a lie. But he had a daughter that he loved beyond all reason. And for her sake, he was going to make some changes.

He was going to cede the field to Crockett.

"This may be the first sound judgment I've had in a while," he told his slumbering lump of a brother. "But I love you. You're a dope, like all of us, but you are my brother, and you would have killed yourself to save me from my own folly."

As Last said it, tears warmed his eyes.

He wanted happiness for his brother. He wanted happiness for his child, and he wanted happiness for Valentine. Nothing else mattered. Under Bloodthirsty's hooves, he'd known Crockett was the first one in the ring to save him. It had been the ultimate gift of brotherhood.

This lesson of sacrifice Last had learned by example, and he'd never forget it. No longer the baby, Last was a different person, and he knew exactly what he had to do.

"THERE," VALENTINE SAID, after she'd hung up the phone, "that takes care of that."

Mimi's eyes were huge. "I'm not sure Crockett knows what to do with female rejection."

"He probably won't remember proposing, but I will always remember that my mind was made up. It's good to have a plan."

"But what if the plan doesn't work?" Mimi asked worriedly.

"He's not in love with me," Valentine

pointed out. "Crockett chases, he teases, he gets moody, but he never shows any emotions. Not really."

"You have to read his actions. That one is deep."

She thought about the round-fannied figurine she'd seen in his kitchen. "Must be very deep. Truthfully, Mimi, I don't think Crockett can care for only one woman. Maybe none of the bachelor brothers can. You know, when I took that birthday cake to Mason, and he pulled out the thong from the center—"

"Thong?" Mimi's face turned pale.

"Yes. I baked it into the cake—Mimi, are you all right?"

Mimi laughed a little nervously. "Of course. Who was the cake from?"

"I don't know. It was anonymous. She paid cash, and I assumed Mason would know who sent it, but he didn't. What's wrong?" Valentine asked, seeing that Mimi looked distressed.

"I'm fine." Mimi shook her head, got

up from the table and began gathering Nanette's things.

"Mimi, have I upset you?" Valentine asked.

"Absolutely not. You are a dear," Mimi said airily. "I'm so glad you have your feet on firm footing where Crockett is concerned. Let me know if there is anything I can do to help you in any way."

"Thank you for stopping by," Valentine said. "I enjoyed our chat."

That brought a slight smile to Mimi's face. "It's wonderful to have another woman around who has a young child. I feel as though we're sisters."

Valentine smiled. "Me, too. The girls will be such awesome friends, I'm sure."

Mimi nodded, kissed Annette goodbye and left with Nanette in her arms. Valentine stared after her, worried.

Something had definitely been on Mimi's mind, something that had to do with the cake. She would never know, of course, what had made her friend suddenly turn pale. Maybe she hadn't been feeling well.

"And on that note," Valentine said to Annette, bending down to gently pull her up, "you and I need to get home. I have some more Father's Day planning to do, and you need a nap, little one. Hopefully, your daddy will feel well enough to picnic."

Crockett, too. Even though she had turned down his proposal, she almost wished it had been a real one. "Your uncle is such a dramatist," she told Annette as she locked up. "Tomorrow, we'll go see your father—you'll be more cheering than a bouquet of flowers and then I need to make a special trip to Delilah's and see if there is any way I can help her. I owe her an apology."

What she wouldn't say out loud to her daughter was that she was looking forward to seeing Uncle Crockett most of all. Because medicine-head or not, he *had* proposed.

Though she tried hard not to admit it,

the moment Crockett had jumped the rail and dashed into the ring to save his brother, he had taken her heart with him.

But she'd been right to turn him down. There was Last, the family's disapproval and Crockett's mystery lady to consider. On top of all that, a woman should have a proper proposal before she decided to spend a lifetime with a man. It didn't have to be on bended knee, but it should be in person, and romantic, and memorable. She wanted her once-in-a-lifetime proposal to be the stuff of dreams. Her sister, Nina, had received a surprise, romantic proposal from Navarro. Their marriage was built on love and respect.

Annette wiggled in her arms and Valentine knew she needed to focus a little less on fairy tales and a bit more on practicality. She wanted a family for her daughter, but only with a man who loved Valentine for the woman she'd become.

"We're going to be brave," she told Annette. "We are going to wait until we know for certain that he is in love with *both* of us."

And if that happened, then she would know she had caught a cowboy worth keeping.

Chapter Twelve

Valentine wasn't expecting it, but at six o'clock the next morning, there was a banging on her front door. Sleepily, she got up to open it, only to find Mason standing there. "Hi," she said.

"I woke you," he replied. "I'm sorry. I thought you'd be up because of the bakery."

"I should be, yes. Come in."

"No, thank you." He cast a glance around inside her living room. "Is Last here, by chance?"

"Last? No. Isn't he in the hospital?"

He grimaced. "He's supposed to be. But he got himself released somehow, and he's gone. Crockett is useless. He has no idea when his brother left."

"They were in the same room," Valentine said. "He would notice his brother packing up and leaving."

"Unfortunately, no. He had an adverse reaction to his medication. Apparently, very adverse." Mason shook his head. "He slept like a man in a coma for a full day."

"Oh. I thought he sounded strange when he called." There was her answer. The proposal had been *all* pharmacology.

"He called you? Did he say anything important?"

"If you mean about Last, he never came up."

"I don't know how Last could disappear like that, but I'm going to pound him when I see him."

Valentine's eyes widened at the sincerity in Mason's tone. He really was worried about him. "Did one of your brothers come by?"

"They wouldn't dare." Mason pursed his lips. "Jerry has been known to bring his truck and conduct a rescue, but he wouldn't have, either. Besides, he's too busy moving Delilah's belongings."

"That leaves a special woman."

Mason looked at her. "The only special woman in Last's life is his daughter. I assume Annette is in her crib?"

"Actually, she slept with me last night. I promise, Last was not here. Though I am surprised he didn't call me."

Mason tipped his hat. "I'll let you know if I hear anything. I'm on my way to pick up Crockett now."

"You are?"

"Sure. Nothing wrong with him that a little Helga-cooking won't cure. Crockett adores her sauerkraut."

Valentine blinked. "Can I help you?"

"Just ring me if you hear from Last. My cell is on."

"I will." She closed the door, frowning. So Last was gone, and Crockett had been out of his head when he'd called her. Great.

When she went back up to her bedroom, Annette sat up in bed, blinking sleepy eyes at her mother. Her hair was tousled and sweet, and Valentine smiled. "You don't know it," she said, "but both of the men in your life have turned out to be duds. One can't handle his medicine and so offers proposals—a very bad sign, I'm sure—and the other has developed a wandering foot. You, my dear, should not look to either of these men for guidance when you are a teenager."

Annette giggled, only understanding that her mother was bouncing her on the bed like a toaster popping toast. The phone rang, and Valentine pointed at her daughter. "Stay right there, okay, sweetie?"

In the kitchen, she found the portable phone and padded back toward her bedroom. "Hello?"

"Valentine," a deep voice said.

"Last?" She halted in her tracks. "Where are you?"

"Never mind that. I need you to keep a secret for me."

"Of course."

"I've gone away to get some R & R."

"Are you all right?"

"Yes. But I'm not planning on coming back for a while. I want you to know, because of Annette. I don't want her to think that…her dad abandoned her."

He was thinking of Maverick. Valentine kept walking and went to sit on the bed so she could stroke her daughter's hair. "I don't understand."

He hesitated. "I just needed to get away. I hated being in the hospital, I hate being laid up, and I didn't want to be a burden to you or my brothers. I decided to take a recuperative vacation."

"For how long? I'm having a Father's Day Picnic in a couple of weeks."

"I won't be back by then," he said. "I'm sorry. But it's really sweet of you to do it."

An uncomfortable feeling ran over her. The sudden disappearance; the excuses about being a burden. "You're not coming back, are you?"

"Not for a long time. I wanted you to know so that Annette wouldn't…think she'd been left, and so you'll know that I'm fine. I've gone off before, but this time, I need to stake my own claim. I'd appreciate you not sharing that with my brothers. I'll call you from time to time to talk to Annette, if you don't mind."

"Of course. But, Last," she said.

"Yes?"

"What does staking your claim mean, exactly?"

"It's really hard to explain," he said, "but I need something that's mine. Something that's not Malfunction Junction."

She, too, had left home to stake her own claim, a long time ago. It was what had brought her to Lonely Hearts Station. But Union Junction was now her home, and she couldn't imagine leaving it.

But she understood how he felt. "I'm glad you told me. I completely understand."

"I knew you would. Valentine, there's something I've been wanting to say to you for a long time. I should say it in person, but now seems the right time."

"All right." She tensed, waiting.

"I'm sorry for the way I treated you. You're a wonderful mother and a great lady. I wish things had been different between us. I wish I was a different person. I'm not the man for you, but I'm glad you and I share a child. Annette's awesome."

Quick tears sprung to Valentine's eyes. "That means a lot. Thanks."

"I think you handle our relationship well. I appreciate the fact that you're always cool with whatever happens. You're rock solid, Valentine, and there was a time nobody knew that, maybe not even you. But you are."

"Call often, Last. Annette will want to hear from her daddy."

"I will. And look after my lout of a brother, okay? He can't hold his drugs worth squat."

She laughed. "So I heard. And nobody looks after you Jeffersons, you know that. But I'll take him an occasional cookie."

"All right. Goodbye."

"Talk to your daughter now." She

handed the phone to Annette, who just sat and listened to her father's voice coming through the earpiece with a big grin on her face. After a moment, when Annette put the phone down, Valentine very softly clicked the phone off.

AT SEVEN O'CLOCK that evening, after Valentine had put a seriously tired and cranky but freshly bathed Annette to bed, another banging on her front door surprised her. With Last being gone, she had decided not to go to Lonely Hearts Station. She didn't want Crockett thinking she'd driven all that way just to see him.

So the best part was opening the door and finding Crockett on the porch.

"Got milk?" he asked. "I'm in the mood for some cookies. And I was wondering if there was a baker in the house."

She blinked. "You're in a cagey mood, aren't you?"

"Just trying to be funny." He waved his crutch goodbye at Jerry, who waved back and then drove away. "Can I come in?"

"It seems that was your original idea."

"Sounds like a plan." He stumped past her and flopped onto the sofa. "It's great to be home."

"Home?" Putting her hands on her hips, she raised a brow. "Have you been into the painkillers again?"

"Oh." He laughed, and she wished he didn't look so handsome in a raffish, mischievous sort of way. Only a Jefferson would look so great fresh from the hospital. "You must be referring to my rambling phone call."

"Maybe."

He waved a magnanimous hand. "I'm here to clear up everything between us."

It would have been nicer if his proposal had merited more serious attention. "I may be a trifle irritated with you."

"Oh, don't be. I've been thinking of you since I woke up. I came right from the hospital just to be here."

"I must say I am surprised."

"Yes. Because you now have a built-in babysitter."

Valentine blinked. "Do I?"

"Yes. And I should probably handle the cooking, since you're not very safe around stoves." He gave her a devilish wink.

"Crockett!"

He laughed. "Hey, you brought up my mistake. I can mention yours in the spirit of…whatever. Now come sit in my lap."

"Let's see, you're offering cooking, babysitting, and other sundry services, as well?"

His grin was huge. "There are a lot of benefits to having me around."

"I don't recall ordering a house husband."

"Try me. You'll like me."

"I don't think so. I'm still annoyed with you."

"I've got a suggestion. Come here." She went and sat next to him, unable to resist his playfulness. "I actually have two suggestions. One, we can watch a movie, or…"

"Yes?"

"You can let me make out with you for the length of time it would take us to watch a movie."

"Wow," she said with big eyes, "you can kiss for two hours?"

"I have other things on tap that last that long, but if you'd like to start with kissing, pucker up and set the egg timer. Is that what you use when you bake? An egg timer?"

"I don't know," she said, sliding into his lap facing him, "do you use an egg timer when you're riding a bull for eight seconds?"

"Nope," he said, letting her knock his hat to the ground. "I use my survival skills alarm."

"I use my touch-it-and-see-if-it-springs-back timer," she said with a teasing smile.

"I like your timer better than mine," he said, rolling her underneath him. "Set it. Starting now."

He kissed her hard and fast and hungrily. This was the way it should have always been—without Last between them.

Valentine was breathless when he pulled away to look at her. "How is your survival skills alarm?" she asked.

"Banging wildly. How is your spring thing?"

"Just about ready to be sprung. Keep going."

He did until Valentine knew that she had never been kissed so thoroughly in her life. Her eyes were teary, her body was on fire, and her desire was raging.

He looked at her. "You like kissing me."

"Yes, I do. Too bad your leg is broken, or you could carry me to my bedroom."

"That's what this crutch is for, making you walk." He picked up his crutch, shooing her along like a shepherd with a sheep. "I did not come all this way not to watch you walk. It's fanny time!"

She turned around, walking backward. "I always suspected you were looking at my bum."

"Lusting is the verb. Turn around."

Turning, she dropped her blouse to the ground.

"Never mind," he said, "you can walk backward if you like."

She smiled. "I'm afraid you're going to hurt something."

"I probably will, but it will be worth it. Plus—" he fell onto the bed with her— "if I can break a leg saving my brother from Bloodthirsty, the very least I can do is hurt something for you."

And then he kissed her, sliding her clothes from her body. Not near as patient, Valentine pulled off his shirt. "You take off your shorts. I'll watch."

He tossed his shorts and boxers to the floor.

"Oh, my," she said.

"If you touch it, you'll know whether it springs back," he said, cupping possessive hands around her breasts.

She gasped. "I think all my baking rules just went out the window."

"Good," he said, sliding into her as he

kissed her, "I want you to forget everything you ever knew besides me."

She couldn't remember anything, Valentine thought, as they lay in bed for the next two hours making love. He made her cry out time and again with pleasure, but the best thing was knowing that he wanted her so much.

CROCKETT AWAKENED TO feel tap, tap, tapping on his arm. At first, he thought the roof had sprung a leak and water must be dripping in. He had Valentine wrapped in his arms so tightly she had to feel like a mummy. If he had his way, he was never letting go of her.

But still, something kept tapping on his arm.

Rolling over, he found Annette staring at him with big eyes. "Hi," he said, wondering what the protocol for this scenario was and hoping he didn't emotionally scar his niece.

Annette showed him her dolly.

"That's nice, sweetie. Why aren't you in bed?"

"Thirsty."

"Okay. I am, too." Gently, he drew a sheet over Valentine's head so Annette wouldn't see the two of them in bed together—that was probably good parenting, wasn't it? "Take Dolly to the kitchen table, and I'll be right there."

She went off obediently. Careful not to awaken Valentine—who had blown his mind with her generous loving—he hopped into his shorts and shirt, grabbed a crutch and went down the hall.

"Okay, Annette," he said. "Water?"

She nodded her head.

"Me, too." He poured them both some ice water and set the glass and sippy cup on the table. She drank hers until it was empty and looked at him with big eyes.

"Aren't you tired at all?"

Annette shook her head. He wasn't tired, either. Being with Valentine had definitely energized his soul. Not knowing what to do, he glanced around the kitchen, noting the pretty lemon color on the walls and the eyelet draperies. "So," he said to Annette. "Feeling tired yet?"

She shook her head.

Well, there was only one thing left to offer, which every good uncle knew was an irresistible magic charm. "How about a story?"

She smiled.

"Got a favorite one?"

Off down the hall she went, carrying a big book back with her.

"The Three Bears and Other Childhood Stories," he read. Out of curiosity, he read the inside flap.

Annette, This was one of my father's favorite things to read to us. I want to read it to you often. Love, Last.

Crockett's eyes teared up as he snuggled Annette closer to his chest. Why had his brother left this beautiful baby? Crockett couldn't help but think Last's disappearance had something to do with the medicine-induced conversation they'd had.

"My father read to us all the time as kids. These were some of his favorites, along with *Beowulf,* and *The Iliad.* I'm honored to be reading words to you that my father read to me. That your father read to you," he added, thinking of Last.

And when Valentine found them in the morning, the two of them were fast asleep under a woolly plaid afghan, the reading lamp on beside them, and their hands clasped together over the pages.

"WAKE UP, SLEEPYHEADS," Valentine said. She put orange juice, pancakes and fruit on the table. "Anybody hungry?"

Annette hopped out of Crockett's lap and went to the table. Valentine smiled at her daughter's tousled head. Crockett followed her, his gaze showing his appreciation of the breakfast. "Mmm," he said. He kissed her temple, and Valentine shivered.

"Actually, you're my fave food, but I

couldn't say that in front of spud," he whispered in her ear. "I like being your house husband."

"You make it sound like sex slave," she whispered back.

"House husband, sex slave—it's all the same to me."

She paused. She liked this new easiness between them, but she needed to know where they stood. She'd realized yesterday she couldn't afford to be flighty in her relationships. "Crockett, do you remember proposing to me?"

"Yeah, I remember," he said sheepishly, as if he hadn't wanted her to bring it up just yet. "Now, we don't have to call that a *proposal,* if you're going to get all huffy on me. We can call it an agreement offer, if you like."

"Agreement offer?" The man was a nut, she decided, and it wasn't all drugs.

"Yeah." He smiled at her. "Marriage is hardly a novel idea. It's a contract between two parties who each need something, and who stand to benefit from—"

"Crockett, I am not hurting financially," she said. "I am not pining for you or any other man. I'm doing fine on my own."

He nodded. "I'm very proud of you."

She put her hands on her hips. "Just for the record, you do remember my *No, thank you?*"

He glanced up at her. "I didn't think you were serious about that. I was thinking the offer was still on the table. I wouldn't have come here otherwise."

"You seemed pretty out of your head when you asked," she said, ignoring the fact that she really liked the look of him sitting at her table across from her happy child. "I rejected your offer outright, the second time you called."

He looked puzzled, and she took a deep breath. "When you called the second time. I said that I wouldn't marry you if you were the last man—"

"Oh. I see," Crockett said. He rose awkwardly, balancing himself on his crutch.

"You see what?"

He shrugged. "I only called you once."

"If you remember proposing, you must remember the rejection," Valentine said.

"No, I don't," he said, hopping to the door, "because I didn't make that second call. Last must have called after I did. He received your rejection. Maybe that's why he left. I don't know. What I do know is how you really feel about marrying me."

Valentine blinked. "Last never asked me to marry him, so he knows he wasn't being rejected."

Crockett opened the door. "But he knows you rejected my proposal. My guess is he thinks he's standing in my way. We brothers tend to be very careful about stepping in each other's business."

"You *thrive* on getting into each other's business," Valentine said.

"But not where women we care about are concerned. So he left. However, apparently, I am the one in the way. You wouldn't marry me if I was the last man in the world?"

"Crockett, wait," Valentine said, but he headed out the door.

"I get it," he said. "Now I get the *whole* picture."

She watched as he crutched off toward the main house. Annette stood beside her, looking up, wondering why Crockett was leaving. Valentine sighed. "Uncle Crockett is fussy because his leg hurts, sweetie."

But Valentine knew the real reason Crockett left. She'd only been trying to clear the air between them and start fresh, but she had hurt his feelings and his pride, and as she saw him in the distance, she wished she could have him back again.

Chapter Thirteen

Nearly fourteen days later, on the day before the belated Father's Day picnic, Crockett found himself still in a wounds-licking mood. His leg was itchy, though not sore. He was, in a word, bored.

Valentine's outright rejection of any commitment where he was concerned had hurt him deeply. Why had she made love with him? How was a man supposed to react when a woman gave her body but not her trust?

He had been convinced that she would want to be with him…once she knew the magic of their shared togetherness.

Valentine stayed far away from their house.

He didn't go to the bakery. Or her house.

He was feeling very disconnected.

The only way he knew to solve that problem was to face his other issue: artistic creation. If Last could run away—blast him—then certainly Crockett could hide out, too.

"Hi," Minnie said, appearing at his elbow as he sat in the barn pondering his boredom.

"Hi," Kenny said. "Are you thinking, Uncle Crockett?"

"Or are you daydreaming?" Minnie asked. "Sometimes Grandpa Barley daydreams with his eyes open. Mom says he's taking a nap, but Grandpa doesn't like for her to call it that."

Crockett could well imagine. "I need a couple of things from you two," he said. "This is a top secret mission."

"Cool," Minnie said. "We're very good at secrets."

He knew they weren't, but it wasn't as though anybody really cared about his life, he thought, engaging in a moment of self-pity. "You remember when you found my painting?"

They nodded.

"Can you bring me my canvas and my paints without telling Mason or Helga or Calhoun or anybody else that I'm setting up my studio out here?"

Minnie looked around. "With the horses?"

"It's quiet, and I can't get up the stairs right now, you know."

She grinned. "Not as easily as we can."

"Precisely. That's why I need you two agile children to get my canvas out here without dropping it down the stairs." He frowned, rethinking his plan.

"I can do it," Valentine said, walking into the barn.

"Uh-oh," Minnie said. "You blew your own secret, Uncle Crockett."

Crockett squelched the happiness he felt at seeing her and told himself she was the reason he was returning to the ol' paintbox.

"I brought cookies," Valentine said.

"Yay!" Minnie and Kenny peered into her basket. "Oh, this one has a broken leg," Minnie said. "It must be yours, Uncle Crockett."

She handed the cookie to him. He took it reluctantly after glancing Valentine's way. She had baked a gingerbread man, with a frosting cast! He gave her a sour look. "No heart on this one."

"I gave up hearts," Valentine said. "They didn't stay on very well."

"Hmm." Was she trying to tell him something? Whatever it was, he didn't care, even if she did bake wonderful cookies. Eating his, he gave her a studied look. She was adorable as always, in a white skirt and a strapless top. Very summery, very cool. Very edible. "Where's spud?"

"With Mimi. She said it was her turn to babysit."

"Ah."

"Have you heard from your brother?" she asked, making certain that Minnie and Kenny both received cookies from the basket.

"All I know is that he talked Hawk into picking him up from the hospital—that's how he escaped. Since Hawk didn't find much on his second Maverick-hunting trip, he was probably looking for a way to help. It should have occurred to me that Last would call Hawk, since he needed someone with some medical knowledge, banged up as he was."

"We're going to go get your canvas now," Minnie said.

"Never mind," Crockett said, not wanting Valentine to be involved in the setup of his new studio. "I've lost the urge to be creative."

"All right. We'll see you later, then. Thanks for the cookies, Aunt Valentine!"

The kids left, running happily across the fields. Crockett wished they'd stayed to protect him from Valentine.

"I'm sorry I hurt your feelings," Valentine said. "You guys act all rough and ready on the outside, but inside you're mushy cream fillings. I forgot that."

"Not true. I'm tough as a rock."

Valentine walked over and gave him a kiss that stole his breath. "Wow," he said, "what was that for?"

"I'm sorry I'm not the woman for you," she said. "It doesn't mean I don't think you're a wonderful man. But what I want and what you want are two different things."

"What do you want?"

"To be loved," she said simply. And then she walked out of the barn.

He stared after her, his jaw slack. "What the hell was that?" She wanted to be loved? Love was a very big leap. He'd wanted to go more slowly, action and then emotion. Truthfully, he was confused.

"Hey," Mason said, walking into the barn. "How's the leg?"

"Is this Grand Central Station and someone forgot to hang the sign?" Crockett snapped.

"Cool your tail, rattler," Mason said mildly. "It was just a simple question."

"I know." But he had his mind on Valentine, and there was nothing simple about her.

"Last will be home tomorrow," Mason said. "He just called. Said he wanted to be here for Valentine's Father's Day picnic."

"How nice."

"Is there something you want to talk about?"

Crockett glared. "Did you become a shrink and didn't tell me?"

"Wow," Mason said. "I must have missed the early-afternoon horror show, Frankie."

"Frankie?" He cocked a brow at his brother.

"Frankenstein?" Mason said sardonically.

"Oh. Whatever."

"You've been quite a jackass ever since Bloodthirsty stomped you."

"Yeah?"

"Yes. And it's getting on my nerves."

"I seem to be getting on everyone's nerves."

"Well, try not to tomorrow. Valentine has put a lot of effort into this for Last's sake."

Crockett frowned. "I'm partially a father."

Mason laughed as he bent to toss some hay over a stall. "I don't think so. You're maintaining favored uncle status, barely. At the rate you're going, your status will soon be lowered."

Crockett sat, smoldering. He could have been elevated, if Valentine hadn't rejected him. Her parting shot didn't sit well with him.

"I thought I saw Valentine crossing the lawn," Mason said.

"She brought me a cookie with a broken leg," Crockett said.

"She's such a nice girl," Mason said. "I heard Widow Fancy's grandson wants to go out with her. He mentioned it to Lily at the Union Junction Salon."

Crockett blinked at the instant *whoosh!*

inside his skull. He pressed on his head, willing it to stay in one piece, but it sure felt as if part of it had popped off. Never had he thought Valentine might date someone other than him or Last! He or Last was fine—well, not Last. But definitely not someone outside of the family!

"What a mess that would be," Crockett said, more gloomy than ever.

"I think you're right. Last probably wouldn't like it a bit."

"Well, then Last better get his trouble-making tail home and defend his territory," Crockett said. "Everything was going along just fine until he decided to prove his manhood on Bloodthirsty. That is when this whole matter began to seriously deteriorate."

Mason glanced at him. "You sound rather disturbed."

"I am!"

"Because of Last, or because of Valentine?"

"I don't know. How's that for an answer? Both, and maybe neither."

"Whew. You do have your britches in a twist."

Crockett grunted. "Identical to yours. You know, Mason, you might have a little sympathy. Your britches were twisted long before any of us wore long jeans, and they're still twisted. Don't act like you have all the answers."

Before Mason could answer Crockett stumped off, wheeling his crutch in a righteous snit. If he could get through the picnic without blowing his cool, he'd be as proud of himself as when he'd ridden Bloodthirsty to the bell.

VALENTINE WAS SITTING in the kitchen at the main ranch house with Helga when Crockett slammed the front door, startling both the women.

"Tsk," Helga said.

"Sorry," Crockett said. "You're still here," he said to Valentine.

"Yes. We're having woman-chat."

"Glad it's not catching," he said.

Valentine frowned. "You're safe."

He hovered in the doorway, apparently not sure if he should interrupt.

"I've been looking at this woman you sculpted," she said, hoping to keep him there a moment longer.

"Yeah?"

"I think she's beautiful."

He hesitated. "I think she's beautiful, too."

"Are you going to do any more?" Valentine allowed her gaze to roam over his stiffly set shoulders.

"I don't think so," he said. "One's best efforts come from the most difficult things one faces. That wasn't difficult. Painting is."

She set the curved feminine sculpture down. "It's too bad. I think you have a calling for nudes."

"Probably. I like them very much."

"All men love nudes. But this one," she said, picking up the sculpture again, "seems like she had a lot of love and thought lavished on her."

He shrugged. "I'm that kind of man. Good to my girls." Then he stomped away.

Trying not to watch him leave, she stood, picking up her now-empty basket. Giving Helga a hug, she said, "I'll see you tomorrow. Thank you for helping me with the picnic."

Helga nodded, her smile happy.

Valentine walked to her car, and before she could get in, Crockett was at her side.

"I just have one question," he said.

"Yes?" Valentine looked up, admiring the glint in his eyes and the mahogany of his sun-touched hair.

"Why are you having a special Father's Day picnic for Last? More than a month after the holiday."

"Because," Valentine said, opening her truck door. "He is Annette's father, and she loves him, and I want her to grow up knowing how to love and respect her father. It's not just for Last—it's for Barley and the sheriff and all the fathers in the family who can be here." She looked

up at him. "Being a father should be celebrated."

"But see, therein lies my issue."

His hand crept up the back of her neck,
and Valentine froze, her heart beating
faster, her body softening in all the right
places. Her emotional resolve melted
away. "Issue?"

"I'm not a father."

"Well—" Valentine didn't really know
what to say to that. "Did you want to be
one?"

"Not last year."

She didn't know what to make of his
soft words so she retreated to familiar territory. "Are you jealous of Last?"

He shook his head, squeezing the back
of her neck. It felt so good to have him
touch her.

"I am not jealous of my brother in any
way."

Suddenly worried, she said, "You are
going to be at the picnic tomorrow?"

"You wouldn't go out with Widow Fancy's grandson?" he asked, surprising her.

"No. Why do you ask such a thing?"

"It's just gossip I heard."

Valentine shook her head. "I own a business. I raise a child, now mainly alone because your brother thinks if he's out of the way you'll romance me."

He didn't say anything.

She sighed. "I don't have time for dating. So I don't know why anybody would be gossiping. Not that it's any of your business."

He kissed her, and Valentine melted against him, grateful that they weren't speaking anymore. It was much better, and easier, to touch him and hold him, rather than try to figure things out.

To her surprise, he pulled away. She looked at him.

"You are the statue," he said, then he walked away.

Chapter Fourteen

Beautiful weather blessed the picnic day. In spite of everything that had happened, Valentine was glad she had done it. The event had turned out quite a bit larger than she had anticipated, since the Jeffersons had told everyone they knew to come on out.

Mason, she suspected, did not like the dwindling feel of the ranch and preferred more people than less.

After her conversation with Crockett, she had decided two things. One, she would try to forget that he'd created a beautiful statue of her. And, two, the special celebration should not be a fathers' event only.

She made two long signs on white

butcher paper, painting them to read, "Happy Man's Day." She put one up in town over her bakery sign and the other she put up at the ranch to greet incoming guests.

"Man's Day," Mimi said with a giggle. "I think Crockett got to you."

"A little." Valentine smiled as she uncovered a blueberry pie on the picnic table.

"I warned you that the brothers can be very convincing."

"He surprised me with his feelings about not being a father," Valentine admitted. "It made me realize that this event should be about grandfathers, uncles and men, like Mason, who are just good men."

"Oh." Mimi looked a little pale suddenly. "I guess so."

"If it goes well, maybe it will turn into an annual event," Valentine said. "So I called it Man's Day, which sounds like a vitamin, but it was the best compromise I could dream up."

"So, does this mean something important is happening between you and Crockett?"

"If you call distinct unease important, I guess so."

"Unease?"

Valentine nodded. "It's just more complicated than I realized it would be. You know, in the beginning I didn't think of Crockett as anything more than one of Last's brothers. It was always a bit awkward for me, because I knew none of the brothers really wanted me here. But my living here seemed to go better than expected."

"And now?"

"Now that any romantic feelings between me and Crockett are such a mess, I miss him. Maybe I shouldn't be feeling the loss of our friendship, but I do."

"Valentine, they're difficult men. No day is only black or white with them."

"I know." Valentine smiled. "I don't regret any of it. But my life needs to go in a different direction now. Frankly, it probably should have sooner, but I had gotten comfortable."

Crockett sat down at the picnic table, glancing up at both the women. "I'm very comfortable now. Look at all this food."

Mimi laughed. "Crockett, you have such a sweet tooth."

He nodded, cutting a piece of pie for himself. "I like the banner you designed, Valentine."

His pointed look made her hesitate. "Well, you gave me the idea."

"It feels very special to be celebrated just for being a man," he said.

Mimi poked his shoulder as she walked by to lay more napkins on the table. "Not like you guys don't celebrate that every single day of your lives."

He laughed. "So, who's getting comfortable?"

"I am," Valentine said. "I've been thinking about some changes."

"Change never makes me comfortable," Crockett said.

"I hate change, too," Last said, coming to sit beside his brother.

"Last!" Valentine beamed, and Annette ran to jump into her father's lap. "I didn't think you'd make it," Valentine said.

"I wouldn't miss a day with my girl," he said, snuggling Annette to him. "Uh-oh, has somebody been in Mommy's perfume?"

Valentine smiled. "Oh, everything I did this morning, she had to do. She's turned into quite a little monkey-see. But, Annette *has* been helping me set up, haven't you?"

Annette nodded, grinning.

"How are you feeling?" Crockett asked Last.

"Damn glad you got me out from underneath that bull," Last admitted. "If you hadn't I might not be here to spend Man's Day with my girl." He wrinkled up his nose. "Man's Day sounds like a libido enhancer."

Valentine laughed. "That's a plus, right?"

"Okay," Last said. "So who's making changes? I walked into the middle of what you were talking about."

"Oh, for heaven's sake," Mimi said. "I hate how you Jeffersons can bounce between three or four conversations."

Last grinned. "Hawk has been healing me with Indian techniques and medicine. That, or we've just been on a major bender for several days. Whatever he's been doing, it's given me amazing powers of focus that I've never had before."

Crockett ate his blueberry pie happily. "I don't care what the subject is, I am going to have a plate of corn and grilled chicken. So, who's changing?"

"I'm not changing, exactly," Valentine said slowly. "I've decided to move into town."

CROCKETT STARED AT Valentine. He lost his appetite for the pie he'd been enjoying. He'd known this would happen. From the beginning, he had realized that romancing Valentine could seriously backfire, and if it did, she would move away from the ranch.

But it wasn't going to be his problem, he decided. If that's what she wanted, fine. Putting his napkin on the table, he stared at her.

Last was silent, too, which surprised him.

"Aren't you going to say anything?" Crockett demanded of Last.

"What?" Last asked defensively. "Does it matter?"

Well, hell, yeah, it mattered. Mimi had moved to town, and that had done nothing for Mason's ability to keep an eye on her. Of course, Mason would never admit that Mimi *needed* an eye kept on her, which was the biggest part of the problem. Crockett's moose-headed brother hadn't realized that sometimes a woman made poor decisions based upon her heart.

So did men, but most of the time they were more logical. "I think it should matter to you," Crockett said slowly. "That's your baby who lives on this Jefferson ranch."

"I can hardly be upset," Last said, cutting himself a piece of pie. "Dessert first, and then dinner, right?" He beamed at Valentine. "Whenever I'm around your baking, all I want to do is eat."

Valentine smiled, sitting down across from him and taking the knife from his hand. She cut his piece of pie, put it on a plate, then handed it to him. "Eat slowly," she said. "Those are awesome blueberries. I got them at a farmer's market, and I don't know if I'll be able to get more of that variety."

Crockett looked at his plate, confused. She hadn't cut his piece! She hadn't given him explicit instructions on how to draw out the gastronomic pleasure!

"Excuse me," Crockett said. "I believe my powers of focus are sharpening just by sitting next to you. Did you say you can hardly be upset that your child who bears the name of Jefferson is moving off Jefferson land?"

Sighing, Last put down his fork. "Crockett, I've been gone for a couple of weeks. Believe it or not, there's something very liberating about being away from Malfunction Junction."

"Liberating?" Crockett thought his ears were going to pop off his head.

Mimi laughed. "Crockett, you're turning the color of that blueberry sauce. Do you need sunscreen?"

None of this conversation suited him. He really felt that his brother should step up to a *different* plate and take care of his responsibilities. If Valentine was *his* woman, she wouldn't be going anywhere.

This was her home. Hers and Annette's.

"Where are you thinking about moving?" Mimi asked.

"I like your setup. You're close to town, in a small abode."

"It's nice," Mimi admitted. "Not so much housecleaning."

"I'll clean your house," Crockett said. "I did offer to be your house husband."

Last turned to him. "What the hell is that?"

Crockett glared at his brother. "I offered to babysit Annette."

"And I thank you," Valentine said earnestly. "But in town, near my bakery, Annette won't need a babysitter. She'll be with me, and when she wants to play, there are other children in town. Other mothers my age. Especially when the Lonely Hearts girls move to town next weekend."

Crockett stared, his heart beginning to race. She had thought this plan through. This wasn't just something she was saying to needle him—er, Last.

"You know," Last said, "though you seem to think I'm dropping the ball by not trying to convince her to stay, you must have dropped a really big ball if she's not dying to live three feet away from you. I mean, usually women are throwing themselves at us. This one, like Mimi, has decided to move away. Best you look to your own method."

Well, that was a fine howdy-doody, Crockett thought. Last's baby and the baby's mother were moving away, and he, Crockett, was the fall guy.

They all looked at him expectantly.

He'd never considered that Valentine might miss the company of other women. Living in town would be a lot better for Annette, actually—but that didn't mean he liked it.

"I could plan to be around to help you move your stuff," Last said, and Crockett blew a fuse.

"Jeffersons stay on Jefferson land," he said.

Last laughed. "Bull. The only Jefferson brothers left here are Mason and you. Well, Calhoun, but he doesn't count, because he's got his own family down at his house, and heaven knows you don't go down there often because you got your pride stirred up over artistic differences. Bandera, who knows when he's going to stop floating around in the sky or where he'll settle. That leaves Valentine living on a *ghost* ranch."

An arrow of remorse buried itself deeply in Crockett's chest. Did no one care that the old ways were disappearing? Everything was going the wrong way, including Valentine. She should have wanted to say yes to his proposal and she should want to live on this fine ranch.

Anger overrode his better judgment. "I get it," he said, standing, "this is all my fault. You and I smooched a little, spent a little time together—which I knew was a bad idea—and now you're going to leave me here to stew in my own juices."

"Bro, I really don't think this is about you," Last said, his tone warning.

"Just go on then," Crockett said to Valentine. "Just go. Get off the ranch, if you want to so badly."

Last stood, stepping away from the bench. "Crockett, shut your mouth."

"I shouldn't have done it. I asked you to marry me, and you didn't want to, and now you're running away from me. Fine." Crockett stood, too, and the two brothers glared at each other eye to eye.

"Don't talk to Valentine that way," Last said.

"That seems funny coming from you, Last, since you spent the first several months she was here wearing a Mohawk and an earring and avoiding your fatherly duties."

Valentine stood between them. She pushed them apart, and then turned to Crockett. "There are many reasons a woman wants change. In this case, it's absolutely imperative that a lot of things in my life be different."

Crockett stared down at her, wondering what he'd done to make her decide to pull up roots. Why would she leave him?

"Was it so very bad?" he asked, his heart paining him.

"It was so very good," she said. "I wanted to be loved. I still do. But that's not what you're offering. And now there's going to be more of me to love. I really have to keep my priorities straight."

"I don't care how plump you get," Crockett said. "Anybody who works in a bakery is going to put on a pound or two. But, Valentine, your booty's always been the best part of you."

She shook her head. "That's not what I meant. Crockett, I'm having a baby."

Chapter Fifteen

Crockett stared at Valentine, dimly aware that Mimi and Last were walking away. There was an emotional boulder sitting on Crockett's chest and something buzzing loudly in his brain. "Baby?"

She nodded. "It's very early, but yes."

"Mine. We're having a baby."

She nodded again. "We didn't use any protection that night. Honestly, I assumed I was at the right place in my cycle."

He didn't know what to say. Half of him wanted to jump up and down and shout. But the other half was cautious. In spite of this good news, she was moving farther away—from him.

"I'm confused," he said finally. "Why are you moving into town?"

"I already told you."

"But I have offered to take care of you."

Valentine took a deep breath. "Crockett, unfortunately, having a baby doesn't change the fundamental problems between us. We're friends, and if you don't love me, then we can't be anything more."

"I think we're past friendship if we're having a baby." He felt very cross about the friendship notion.

"Last and I are friends. And perhaps if you'd understood that in the beginning—"

"I am allowed a bit of familial jealousy," Crockett said. "It didn't really have anything to do with you."

"It had everything to do with me. I understood that Last was a bit possessive of his child—"

"But now I'm having a child, and it's my turn to be possessive, and I don't want you moving to town!" He told himself to calm down. "I realize I am probably not saying this properly, but my child should live on this ranch where his heritage is."

"I've picked out the cutest little town-house next to Mimi's," she said.

"Mimi is such a bad influence! She always has been," Crockett grumbled. Sitting down, he drummed his fingers on the table. "I am having a baby," he said. "Me, Crockett Jefferson. I am going to be a father." He perked up. "Hey, I will always be able to celebrate Father's Day!"

Valentine sat across from him. "Now you want it to be Father's Day instead of Man's Day?"

"None of us liked thinking about Father's Day before," he said. "Because of Maverick."

Valentine's lips parted, in a way he greatly appreciated. "I never thought about that," she said. "Of course Father's Day wouldn't have the happiest of memories for you guys."

"Well, we have happy memories. But we can't get away from the fact that we never knew what happened to our father. We appreciated the fact that you were living in the present, Valentine. Now I will always smile on Father's Day. I cannot wait to hold my own bundle of joy."

He felt tears pop into his eyes as he thought about it. Had Maverick felt this way? He remembered his father's firm hands guiding him along a path of steadfast love and companionship. "I'm going to be a helluva dad," he said. "I've got to brush up on my Latin." He gave her a sideways glance. "You sure you don't want to get married?"

"I'm not sure about anything. I can't believe I'm pregnant again."

"Are you happy?" Despite the snarl in their relationship, Crockett really wanted her to be happy about the baby.

"Even though it wasn't in my plan, I am. And I hope it's a little brother for Annette." She bit her lip, then smiled at him. "I hope it's a boy who is just like you."

"You'll give me compliments, but you won't take my ring." He sighed.

"You're a good man, Crockett, and you take your responsibilities very seriously, whether it's saving Last or saving me. I just don't want to be a responsibility."

"I don't have to break anything to save *you*," he said, feeling a bit annoyed.

"I have a present for you," Valentine said.

"Twins?"

She laughed. "No."

"Oh. Because I don't think you can give me anything better than a baby."

In front of him, she placed a cowboy cookie with his name on it. It wore chaps, spurs and a huge hat. "He's got his heart," Crockett observed.

"A big one, too. This is my new design," she said proudly. "I created super-cookie-glue. I'm very proud of it. And it's tasty."

"This is a very studly cookie. You're going to sell a ton of these, especially for bachelor parties and holidays. I can't eat it, though, because I'm going to keep it."

"I made a design for every brother, and the kids. At Christmas, the family will have matching stockings and personalized cookies."

He wanted to cry. "Valentine, you are part of this ranch. You need to stay here."

"Cowboy, you do not handle change well."

"No, I don't. I don't think I'll fit into a townhouse too well."

"Fit?" she asked, her brow raised.

"Fit," he said with a nod. "With this baby, our relationship has moved into a brand-new phase. Neither friendship nor commitment."

"What does that mean?" she asked, laughing.

"It means whither goes my baby, so go I. Or in simpler terms, I'm going to stick on you like this heart on this cookie. If I have to use your super-cookie-glue to keep you stuck to me, then I will steal your secret recipe. That's the new plan," he said. "Change is just a matter of being willing to change again. And I think I'm going to like you introducing change into my life."

SO THIS WAS A JEFFERSON in hot pursuit, Valentine thought, as she carried a plastic container of muffins into her bakery. Crockett held the door open for her, not allowing her to carry anything that weighed more than eight ounces. "Thank you," she said, "although may I just say that I'm only a few weeks pregnant, and I'm not exactly high risk, either."

"And you shouldn't become risky," he said cheerfully. "Now, let's go see this cute little townhouse you picked out."

She sighed. "Shouldn't you be resting your leg?"

"Not bothering me a bit."

"All right. But first I need to take down the Man's Day sign on the bakery."

"Every man in town appreciated you celebrating them," Crockett said, "but in the future, you're only going to celebrate me."

She frowned at him. "Excuse me, have I met this pigheaded side of you before?"

He laughed. "Some ladies would call it romantic."

She pulled out a ladder. He sprang to take it from her. "No more of this for you." Frowning, he said, "I wonder if being in a bakery all day around hot ovens is good for your pregnancy."

"Crockett!" Valentine glared at him. "You are swiftly becoming a pain."

"It will get better as you get accustomed to a man helping you."

"I don't know. You're not going to get up on that ladder with a hurt leg, are you? I put the sign up, I can take it down."

"I have to make certain you're safe. You have a bun in the oven, you know," he said cheerfully.

"That was a very sorry, corny attempt at humor." She put her hands on her hips. "Crockett, I'm not going to like you being stuck to me like glue. I don't think this Jefferson hot pursuit is my cup of tea. Mimi made it sound like it would be so wonderful, but I think it may be overdone."

He stared at her, his jaw slack. She could tell he was truly puzzled.

"Excuse me," a voice said, as the bakery door opened behind her. A tiny wizened face peeked in.

"Come in," Valentine said. "Welcome."

"My friends and I were wondering about your sign on the bakery. I'm Helen Granger from Tulips, Texas. This is my friend, Pansy Trifle. Our other friend, Holt—our town hairdresser—is across the street at the Union Junction salon getting some tips from the girls over there."

Valentine smiled. "What can I do for you?"

"We saw your sign and we wondered what you thought about your Man's Day," Pansy said. "Did you enjoy it?"

Valentine looked at Crockett. "Did you?"

"I didn't think I would," Crockett said, "but actually, I did."

Valentine lifted her chin at him. He liked her spirit, he had to admit.

"We think we would like to incorporate a Ladies Only Day in Tulips," Helen said.

"Maybe monthly," Pansy said.

"Man's Day is once a year, which is all I can take," Crockett said. "But a Ladies Only day is something I'm sure my brothers would love to take part in."

"Really?" Valentine said to Crockett. "And what would they like about Ladies Only?"

"Well, a person can't be sexist," Crockett said. "And it would only make men more curious if there is a town day for ladies. My brothers and I would be there in a snap."

Helen and Pansy clapped their hands.

Valentine glowered at him. "Really?"

"Really," Crockett assured her. "I mean, what do you think?"

"I think," Valentine said, "that Mason isn't the Ladies Only Day type."

"You have a point," he said.

"And I would have hoped that *you* weren't."

Ah. She had him there. But the funny thing was, he was enjoying seeing her get her feathers ruffled a little. She wanted to complain about his jealousy and his possessiveness, but it didn't hurt her at all to wear the shoes he'd been walking in. "I think Ladies Only Day is a fabulous idea," he told Helen and Pansy. "If you decide to institute it, Valentine will supply the baked goods."

Valentine glared at him.

"I will happily deliver the baked goods to Tulips for you. We're going to love taking part. Aren't we, Valentine?" he asked with a grin.

VALENTINE HAD BEEN giving him the silent treatment ever since he'd given her a slight tweaking about Ladies Only Day. She also hadn't been pleased when he'd climbed up the ladder and torn down her Man's Day sign. She didn't need to be on a ladder, but she had insisted he was the one who shouldn't be climbing anything.

He had to admit, it had been risky. But his leg or his baby—hands down, he'd rather risk his leg. It was healing nicely, anyway.

About twenty times an hour, he said to

himself, *I'm going to be a father.* It was this wonderful repetition that he would never tire of hearing.

Until he'd met Valentine, he wasn't aware of his own longings for a child.

What she didn't know was that he'd developed an even stronger, more intense longing—for her. She thought she was getting away from him, but in fact, she was going to run right into his arms. This girl was tricky, he knew, with her pear-shaped bottom and her scared heart. She'd turned him down because she'd thought he was pharmacologically-impaired, according to Mimi. And his brother had skewed her trust in relationships.

But her rejection didn't bother him so much now that he knew the truth. He was in love with her. And she needed him, really needed him, and he was going to convince her that he needed her, too.

Today, he was helping her move her things into the cute little townhouse. It wasn't big—he felt as if he might bump his head every time he moved—but he had a plan for that, too.

Her bed, though, was just right. It was the bed they'd made the baby in. Amongst all this change it had stayed the same. It had the same bedspread, the same pillows.

"And it's going to have me in it," he said with a grin.

"What?" Valentine said.

"Never mind," he said. "I really like your new place."

"You do?" Valentine looked at him suspiciously. "I thought you were opposed to me moving."

"But now I've changed," he said. "See how easy that was?"

Valentine walked over to him. "Crockett, I do not trust you. You are in a very slippery mood, and I warn you, Mimi's told me all about you Jefferson men when you decide to have your way with a woman."

He gave her his most wounded expression. "I am the most innocent of parties."

"And that makes me even more worried. But," Valentine said with a smile, "look how pretty this all is. I love it here!" She turned to him. "Thank you for being helpful and understanding."

There was a knock on her front door, and Valentine smiled at Crockett. "My first visitor."

She opened the door. The locksmith stood outside with keys in his hand. She reached to take the keys, but he handed them to Crockett instead.

"Here are your keys," he said. "All new locks."

"You put new locks on my house?" she asked.

Crockett held up his keys proudly. "These are my keys, to my new townhouse. Next door. Come see my new place."

Disbelieving, she followed him, watching him open the door. "Perfect," he said to the locksmith. "Thank you."

The door swung open, and Valentine gasped. It was an artist's studio, with easels and clay and everything an artist needed to feel at home. She even thought she spied a potter's wheel and some glass-blowing materials.

"I needed a place where I could create in peace," he said. "The attic wasn't really working out with my leg. And Mason had figured out that I was eyeing the barn. So this is my new lair, complete with a lock to keep my brothers out and my creativity in."

Valentine couldn't figure out if she was happy or worried that he intended to be so close to her. It was as if she hadn't moved off the ranch after all!

Part of her was very excited that he intended to be so much a part of her life. She'd never had a man pay her so much attention.

"And this," Crockett said, "is my crowning glory."

He swung open a door, revealing a room full of baby things. A colorful crib, a ton of toys, a carton of diapers, even a measuring chart on one wall.

Valentine slowly turned to face Crockett.

"When you're working, the baby can be here," he explained.

"It sort of feels like I never moved away from you," she said, "and my goal was to rely on myself."

"No, your goal was to not let another Jefferson hurt you. I proposed badly, and now I have some work to do." He took a deep breath. "Right now it's two small houses, but I hope they will eventually grow into one big house. And when you're ready, I intend to knock out the wall that separates us."

Chapter Sixteen

Valentine stared at the determined cowboy, her heart filling with a feeling that she had never had before. "It's a beautiful studio," she said, "though I think I'm mad at you."

"Be mad *about* me," he said. "I swear I'm worth it."

"Do you have any other secrets you're keeping from me? This one was a biggie."

He shook his head. "If I told, it wouldn't be a secret. But I wouldn't let my guard down for an instant if I were you. It's gonna be shady around here for a while. You handle surprise much better than I thought you would."

"Oh, yeah?" She gave him a very demure look.

"You can tell me anything. Tell me you're having twins, tell me you want me to redecorate, but just don't tell me you're never going to be my girl."

"Well, I don't know about being your girl," she said. "The jury is still out on that. I have to wait and see what kind of neighbor you are."

He grinned. "Figures."

"However, I believe there's one more thing you haven't done properly, besides apologize. It's important to know how compatible we are as neighbors before this—"

His cell phone rang, interrupting them. "Excuse me," Crockett said. "It's the family calling. Something you'll have to get used to. They always intrude at the worst time."

She nodded. "No surprise there."

"Hello?" He listened for a few moments. "Great. I can help her." He hung up. "Delilah is on her way to town with Jerry's truck loaded full of her belongings. Mason wants me to help them unload."

"I can help, too."

"No, you can't," Crockett said.

"I can carry lamps!"

"You can't even run a vacuum. You may take a cookie platter over, though. I love your cookies."

Valentine pursed her lips. "We have to get something straight. Just because you live next door to me doesn't mean you own me."

The smile slipped off his face.

"My location has nothing to do with it. The fact that you're having my baby—"

"Does not mean you own me, either."

Crockett frowned. "If you think I'm going to start my fatherhood the way Last started his, you're heading for disappointment."

"Did your father boss your mother around?"

"Oh, no," Crockett said. "My mother did everything she could to please my father. He never had to ask for a thing."

"Oh, boy," Valentine said. "I think we need neighbor counseling."

"Neighbor counseling?"

"Yes. As a reader of classics, you may have come across Robert Frost's opinion of neighborliness in his poem 'The Mending Wall.' One gets a very clear picture of how important it is to set boundaries in the beginning, in order for everyone to coexist peacefully." She smiled. "Having a librarian for a sister comes in handy."

He raised a brow in the manner which she'd dubbed Jefferson cocky. "Personally, I prefer Oscar Wilde's fairy tale, *The Selfish Giant,* and what the giant learned about walls." He grinned broadly. "Having a father who knew how to make his woman happy comes in handy, as well. I'm looking forward to reading the classics he read to us to my own children. Valentine, I will be knocking down this wall eventually."

"Okay, and at that time, we'll go into counseling for men who knock down walls."

His laugh was confident and deeply amused and happier than she'd ever heard it. He crossed his arms and leaned against the very wall he said would one day disappear. "Valentine Cakes, soon to be Jefferson, every misconception and everything you think you know about me is about to change. In fact, I am a cowboy chameleon. And you, my lush-bottomed, pear-shaped sweetie, you are going to *beg* me to tear down this wall. I *promise* you that."

TWO WEEKS LATER, the new Union Junction hairstylists were moved in. Valentine was settled in her new place. Crockett was quite content in his new abode, though he still traveled to the ranch regularly to help out. The artist in him loved having peace and quiet and privacy in which to create. He was letting all his ideas run wild. Painting, glasswork, sculpting. It was as if he suddenly had permission to be himself.

He loved it.

Fueling this surge of creativity, he felt certain, was the little woman next door, whom he was ignoring. Every day he got up, went to the ranch to work, and came home in the evening to create. He made his social rounds, visiting Minnie and Kenny, and the stylists who now resided in Union Junction, but he never darkened the door of Baked Valentines. Nor did he speak to Valentine.

He hadn't given up on making her his. He was just letting her get used to him, biding his time.

He was more productive now than he'd ever been in his life. More ranch work was done, and more creations flowed from him. He was happier, friendlier, more outgoing. No more moodiness.

There were two reasons for that. One, he was filled with determination to create as much art as he possibly could. He'd let bitter feelings overtake him for far too long. Before the baby was born, he intended to find his new groove. Becoming a father-to-be had unleashed his creativity in a way he could never have imagined.

But the other reason for his energy was Valentine. He loved the sound of her front door opening and closing every morning at 4:00 a.m. as she went to work. It was his own personal alarm clock. He'd set his bed against the adjoining wall of her bedroom, and he knew when she showered, and when she left.

When he heard that lock spring closed for the day, he jumped out of bed and into his clothes, racing to work at Malfunction Junction. His whole day seemed lighter and more carefree now that he lived next door to his lady.

He also discovered that she loved to sing rockabilly to herself and to Annette, and not very well, either, which made him laugh. The two of them could make quite a ruckus. And when they got started with the pots and pans, it was outrageous. He figured he was the only neighbor who could put up with the banging duet.

At night, when everything was done,

he stayed up in his studio, lit only by a soft lamp and some track lighting, indulging his artistic passion.

One day his life would include his grandest passion. Valentine wasn't quite ready for that, but if there was one thing Crockett possessed in abundance, it was patience.

VALENTINE WAS STARTING to lose her patience. She and Crockett had been neighbors for more than two weeks, and he hadn't so much as called her. He was so quiet over there that it was getting on her nerves. She and Annette had pot-banging parties and he never called to complain. They opened the windows and let the good smell of baking muffins waft out, but he never took the bait.

If this was Jefferson romance, it was pretty annoying.

Maybe he'd changed his mind.

Perhaps he regretted moving away from the ranch. But anytime someone mentioned him, he seemed to be doing well. He'd been everywhere.

Hearing whispers and shushed giggling, she raced to peer out her front window. Her eyes widened. There was a line of women going into Crockett's townhouse! At least twenty of them.

He had not invited her over there since the day he'd gotten new locks, and he certainly had not mentioned a party!

"Spying never hurt anything," she said, peering back out the window. What was he doing now? "Okay, this is not what Mimi said it would be like. This is not Crockett romancing me down to my sandals." She sat on the sofa, thinking things over.

She had told him no.

So he was free to see other women. "Many other women, apparently," she murmured. And of course with all the new ladies in town, there were plenty to choose from.

"He said I would beg him to knock down the wall between us." Surely he hadn't meant he'd make her beg by making her jealous?

"Because that won't work," she said. "Annette, you and I are going to change into our jammies, and then we're going to read a story together, while Mr. Party Jefferson over there has a wonderful time entertaining in the studio that was *supposed* to be his private lair. Apparently, not private when it comes to females, however."

This all made her more worried than she cared to admit. Plus she was getting a wee bit poochy, something she couldn't blame on the bakery. It was all baby. The doctor had said she was right on schedule.

Her doorbell rang, so she gave up worrying to answer the door. Crockett grinned at her. "Hi."

"Hello, Crockett."

"How are you feeling?" he asked.

Oh, jealous, annoyed, unattractive. "Fine. Just dandy," she said airily. "Annette and I are about to go to bed, actually."

"I was hoping you could come over for a while."

A pleased, relieved feeling rose inside her. "I would love to. Can I bring something?"

"Just yourself. We're having a little…"

"Housewarming?"

"Exactly," Crockett said. "Join us when you can."

"Give us five minutes." She closed the door, then raced to brush her hair. "Annette! We're invited after all! Perhaps last minute, but those invitations count, too, don't they! Let's put some pretty clam diggers on you, and maybe a bow in your hair, and lipstick for me."

They got ready quickly and a moment later rang Crockett's doorbell. "I'm here," she said when he opened the door. "And so is Annette."

He took her hand and pulled her inside. "Surprise!"

Annette shrieked and clung to her mother's leg. Valentine laughed, picking up her daughter, and gasped when she saw the sign on the wall that read *Congratulations, Valentine and Crockett!*

"Thank you so much!" she said, still laughing from the shock of it. There had to be forty people packed in the room. All the Union Junction girls and the men from Malfunction Junction—everyone was there. "Is this…did you plan this?" she asked Crockett.

"It was Lily's idea to do the shower," Crockett said, mentioning the manager of the Union Junction salon. "And I wanted to do it here. It seemed like the right place."

"Thank you," she said to everyone. "Thank you so much for thinking of me."

As she looked at all the smiling faces wishing her well, Valentine stopped to take in the memory that she would always hold dear: for the first time in her life, she was part of a circle of friends and family who believed that Valentine Cakes deserved their love.

"This is the most special thing that has ever happened to me, besides my children," she whispered to Crockett. "Thank you so much."

"You deserve it," he said. "You are a truly admirable woman. I'm crazy about you."

Valentine smiled. There were balloons throughout the room and colorfully wrapped presents and a lot of food, but best of all, she realized now, was that she was with him. "Do you remember when you said change was the main ingredient we needed in our relationship?" she asked him.

"I said something like that," Crockett said, "but I'm always babbling."

"Never go away from me again."

He hugged her to him. "You wanted space. I wanted you to have it. But I was keeping an eye on you."

Last walked over, giving her a kiss on the cheek. "Congratulations. I'm happy that Annette will have a little sister."

"Brother," Crockett said. "You have the girls, and I'll have the boys."

"Easy, fellows," Valentine said with a laugh.

"It's okay," Last said. "We have something we want to tell you."

"All right." Valentine and the two men stood close together so that their conversation was private.

"We didn't always make you as comfortable at Malfunction Junction as we could have," Last said. "Initially, we got into a bit of bickering. But we want you to be happy, whether you live here or at the ranch. Your home is with the Jeffersons."

"Thank you," Valentine said. "That means a lot to me."

"All right," Crockett said. "Enough of the mushy stuff. You have a lot of presents to open, and I have a bunch of food to eat."

"I'll join you," Valentine said.

"First open your presents," Mimi called.

"Should I?" Valentine asked.

"Yes!" Lily pulled her over to the sofa, seating Valentine with Annette next to her.

"Lots of diapers," someone said.

"I'm sure." Valentine laughed. "Crockett, come sit with me and Annette. You need to open these diapers, too."

"All right." He sat next to her, and for the next hour, they opened a ton of baby gifts: blankets, silver spoons and a bib that said *Howdy Y'all*.

"Last box," Mimi said, "and I have no idea who it's from because it has no tag. It must have fallen off."

"Oh," Crockett said, swiping the package. "Sorry. That's not for the baby shower."

Valentine looked at him.

He shrugged.

She wanted to slap the smug look off his face.

Two could play at that game. "It's so small," she said, looking at the pretty silver wrapping. "I know what it is."

"You do?" Crockett asked.

"I do. It's one of those little tooth holders. Or maybe a very tiny spoon."

"It's a gift to myself," Crockett said.

"And I'm not telling anybody what I bought."

The ladies groaned and tossed ribbons at him, but he laughed and went into the kitchen to get a plate of food. Valentine stacked the gifts and thanked everyone, but her mind was on the cowboy and his secret.

After giving her space, he was working on her curiosity now. That was going to unravel her.

"I'm taking Annette with me," Last said. "You and Crockett are going to have a lot of cleaning up to do." He kissed Valentine on her cheek and departed, holding his little girl.

"I should go, too," Mimi said, "Isn't that the point of having a party? To make as big a mess as possible for the new parents to clean up?"

"No," Lily said with a laugh.

But cleaning wasn't on Valentine's mind. "Delilah," she said. "Could I talk to you for a second?"

"Certainly." The two women went to one corner of the large room.

"I've never had a chance to tell you how sorry I am that I caught your kitchen on fire," Valentine said. "It was so silly of me."

Delilah smiled. "It was time for me to make some changes. Both in the kitchen and in my life. I wish you would just forget about it and be a happy new mother."

Valentine nodded. "Thank you. If you would accept it, I'd like to give you full use of my bakery kitchen anytime you'd like. I know you can bake in your new place, but there's something very relaxing about a kitchen with all the proper utensils and containers and cake molds. I know how much you love to bake."

"Actually, I would love that. Thank you." Delilah beamed. "It means a lot to me."

Valentine smiled. "I'm glad we ended up on the same side of the street."

Delilah linked her arm through Valentine's, leading her back to the guests.

"You gave Marvella and me a reason to tear down a long-standing wall between us. I'm very grateful."

Valentine smiled, seeing the honesty in Delilah's eyes. Then a guest pulled Valentine away to say good-night, and others headed out the door. Valentine felt as if she was saying goodbye to one of the best nights of her life.

Crockett had been so sweet to arrange this surprise party.

After all the guests left, Valentine couldn't stand it another second. She pounced on Crockett. "You've been keeping secrets."

"Nope. Just one."

"What is it?"

He looked at her strangely. "The party, of course. It's very hard to plan such a thing when you live next door and peer out peepholes."

"I do no such thing!" He was far and away the most elusive man. "Just occasionally."

He laughed. "You sing rockabilly when you think no one is listening."

"And you make no noise at all."

Walking over to the pile of gifts, he said, "I wish the baby would arrive tomorrow."

"You'll have to be patient."

"I hope you can be," he said, waving the silver box at her.

Valentine blinked. "Are you always going to be difficult?"

"You could just say yes," he said, his voice silky.

"I'm not sure about the question." There had been many questions in their relationship.

"Let's start with…come back to my bed."

She felt her cheeks go pink. "Your bed?"

"You've never seen my bedroom. You might like it."

"In a designer sort of way?"

"I don't think so." He took her hand and pulled her back toward his room. As they walked, he wrapped a silver ribbon around her wrists like handcuffs.

"You're a little freaky," she told him.

"It's a good thing. Trust me."

It was a game and all in fun, and Valentine told herself to breathe deeply and put herself in a trusting spirit.

"Kiss me," he said, "and you get a wish."

"A wish?"

He nodded, his eyes glinting.

She kissed him thoroughly and he pulled her down on the bed with him, the silver ribbon keeping her hands together.

"I see you in my room," he said.

She looked at him. "Do you?"

He trailed a finger down her face. "Yeah. Check it out."

She glanced over her shoulder. On the wall was the most beautiful painting she had ever seen. She sat in a wicker chair, her lips curved in a smile, her eyes wide-open and loving as she looked at…

"I'm looking at the artist," she said. "I'm looking at you."

"It's how I see you," he said.

"Make love to me," she said. "My only wish."

He stripped off her clothes and laid her gently on the bed, teasing her with the silver ribbon and kisses. She had almost forgotten how well their bodies fit together, and when he rocked against her a certain way, she cried out her pleasure and wondered how she could have told him no about anything. They lay together holding each other in shared bliss.

Twenty minutes later, when she could breathe, Valentine opened her eyes. Crockett was looking down at her.

"What?"

Gently, he tied the silver ribbon around her neck. "You look like a satisfied kitten," he said. "And a sexy one at that. I want you always in my bed."

"If you bring me another piece of silver ribbon," she said, "I'll tie one on you."

"Tie me up, did you say?"

"No," she said, laughing. "People tie

bows on their fingers to help them not forget things."

He smiled, and kissed her deeply. Then he snapped his fingers. "I did forget something!"

"See? I knew you needed a bow."

He handed her the silver box. "A little housewarming gift," he said.

She tore it open. "It's a key."

"To my house. In case you ever want to visit me."

"Thank you," she said.

"I have to go. I have something I need to do," he said.

"Now?"

Valentine didn't like the sound of that. Reluctantly, she rose and dressed as he did. Then she followed him onto the back patio that adjoined hers. He strode toward his truck without looking back.

Sudden worry struck her. What if he left her?

This man had tempted her, teased her and kept her in a veritable frenzy. She'd had her space; now she wanted him. She knew exactly what the Jefferson males were capable of when it came to making ladies wait. And she wasn't the waiting type, she decided.

She went running after him, catching him as if he were the escaping gingerbread man, only she didn't stop at catching him. She landed on his back, kissing his face and his ears and giving him a rather unladylike kick to the rump.

Laughing, he pulled her around to face him.

"Never do that again," she said.

He tried to look innocent.

"I'm not falling for it," she said. "I figured out the CJ on the fanny of that naked lady. It's your initials, on my fanny. Don't play hard to get."

Then she kissed him. "I am not letting you go," she said. "I've lost too much in my life not to know that sometimes, this time, I've got to hang on as tight as I can, just like you do when you're on Bloodthirsty Black. And I'm hanging on to you."

Crockett grinned. "I like you from your fanny to your sass," he said, grinning. "And I wasn't leaving. I was only going out to my truck to get something."

"To get what?" Valentine demanded, not believing him.

He pulled a big blue velvet box from the truck bed, handing it to her.

She gave him a suspicious stare. It was too big to be a ring.

Opening it slowly, she gasped.

Inside was a gingerbread man with the initials C and V and A entwined with one big J in frosting.

"We're going to be one happy family," he said.

Tears jumped into her eyes. "I did think you were leaving me," she admitted.

"This says I never will." Crockett gave her a tiny box, so small she could cup it in her hand.

Inside was a gorgeous diamond, surrounded by sprinkles and red hots that spilled out as she removed the ring in wonder. "It's beautiful. It's better than beautiful. Tear down the wall," she whispered. "I want to share my life with you."

Crockett slipped the ring on her finger, and as he did, he felt the magic inside him that he always knew he would feel if he ever managed to make this woman his.

And now she was.

"Sweets for the sweet," he murmured to Valentine, before kissing his chosen bride lovingly, and deeply, and far longer than his heart had dreamed possible just a few short months ago.

It was Crockett's final seduction as a bachelor cowboy, but just the first seduction of his forever Valentine.

Epilogue

Valentine did not want a large wedding, but by the time all the Jeffersons and their friends were invited to the ranch, the event could only be called huge. Her groom was happy because all his brothers were in town, with their wives and children. Crockett was very handsome, she thought proudly, in his jeans, crisp white shirt, best black hat and boots.

She was especially happy because Nina was her matron of honor. They giggled like schoolgirls, and Annette dropped white rose petals on the lawn aisle. Valentine was very proud of her daughter.

It was the perfect wedding.

And when Crockett kissed the bride the

joy of the moment brought happy tears to her eyes.

"I don't think you'll be needing the charmed heirloom baby-making bed," Nina whispered at the reception table. "You seem to do quite well without it."

Valentine smiled. "You'll be an auntie again. This time to a boy. Crockett is going to have his own miniature Jefferson cowboy to dress up in boots and a hat." She gazed at her good-looking husband, watching as he watched her. "I never thought I'd be so happy."

"Excuse me, Nina," Crockett said, coming to take Valentine's hand. "My bride and I have an escape to make."

Laughing, they outran the birdseed being thrown their way and jumped into a waiting limo.

"To the airport," Crockett said.

"To France for our honeymoon," said Valentine. "What a wonderful idea. And Annette is so excited about going to visit Nina and Navarro's farm while we're gone."

"I'm looking forward to you coming home with some French culinary secrets," Crockett said, "to add to your skill in the kitchen."

"While I, my love, greatly anticipate you rounding out your knowledge of—"

He raised a brow at her wickedly. "They do say Paris is the city for lovers. And I will be loving you thoroughly."

Valentine smiled. "I was going to say that I greatly anticipate you furthering your appreciation of art at the Louvre. However, if you insist upon staying in your hotel room during your entire stay in the City of Romance—"

He kissed her, silencing her teasing. "I love you," he said.

"And I love you." She smiled, pulling a length of silver ribbon from her bodice. "I brought the handcuffs."

He grinned, pulling a small can from his jacket pocket. "I figured I'd do some painting while we're honeymooning."

"Chocolate body paint," she said, surprised. "Mmm, a working honeymoon for you."

"I'm thinking rosebuds all over your fanny," Crockett replied, pulling Valentine into his lap. And the limo took them toward their future.

* * * * *

YES! Please send me the *Cowboy at Heart* collection in Larger Print. This collection begins with 3 FREE books and 2 FREE gifts in the first shipment, and more free gifts will follow! My books will arrive in 8 monthly shipments until I have the entire 51-book *Cowboy at Heart* collection. I will receive 2 or 3 FREE books in each shipment and I will pay just $4.99 U.S./ $5.89 CDN. for each of the other four books in each shipment, plus $2.99 for shipping and handling.* If I decide to keep the entire collection, I'll have paid for only 32 books because 19 books are FREE! I understand that by accepting the 3 free books and gifts places me under no obligation to buy anything. I can always return a shipment and cancel at any time. My free books and gifts are mine to keep no matter what I decide.

256 HCN 0779   456 HCN 0779

Name _____ (PLEASE PRINT)

Address _____ Apt. #

City _____ State/Prov. _____ Zip/Postal Code

Signature (if under 18, a parent or guardian must sign)

Mail to the **Harlequin® Reader Service:**
IN U.S.A.: P.O. Box 1867, Buffalo, NY 14240-1867
IN CANADA: P.O. Box 609, Fort Erie, Ontario L2A 5X3

Reader Service.com

Manage your account online!

- Review your order history
- Manage your payments
- Update your address

---

*We've designed
the Harlequin® Reader Service
website just for you.*

Enjoy all the features!

- Reader excerpts from any series
- Respond to mailings and
  special monthly offers
- Discover new series available to you
- Browse the Bonus Bucks catalog
- Share your feedback

Visit us at:

ReaderService.com

REQUEST YOUR FREE BOOKS!
2 FREE WHOLESOME ROMANCE NOVELS
IN LARGER PRINT
PLUS 2
FREE
MYSTERY GIFTS

⋇⋇⋇⋇⋇⋇⋇⋇⋇⋇⋇⋇⋇⋇⋇⋇⋇⋇⋇⋇⋇⋇⋇⋇⋇⋇

HEARTWARMING™

❉❉❉❉❉❉❉❉❉❉❉❉❉❉❉❉❉❉❉❉❉❉❉❉❉❉

Wholesome, tender romances

YES! Please send me 2 FREE Harlequin® Heartwarming Larger-Print novels and my 2 FREE mystery gifts (gifts worth about $10). After receiving them, if I don't wish to receive any more books, I can return the shipping statement marked "cancel." If I don't cancel, I will receive 4 brand-new larger-print novels every month and be billed just $4.99 per book in the U.S. or $5.74 per book in Canada. That's a savings of at least 23% off the cover price. It's quite a bargain! Shipping and handling is just 50¢ per book in the U.S. and 75¢ per book in Canada.* I understand that accepting the 2 free books and gifts places me under no obligation to buy anything. I can always return a shipment and cancel at any time. Even if I never buy another book, the two free books and gifts are mine to keep forever.

161/361 IDN F47N

Name	(PLEASE PRINT)	
Address		Apt. #
City	State/Prov.	Zip/Postal Code

Signature (if under 18, a parent or guardian must sign)

Mail to the **Harlequin® Reader Service:**
IN U.S.A.: P.O. Box 1867, Buffalo, NY 14240-1867
IN CANADA: P.O. Box 609, Fort Erie, Ontario L2A 5X3

* Terms and prices subject to change without notice. Prices do not include applicable taxes. Sales tax applicable in N.Y. Canadian residents will be charged applicable taxes. Offer not valid in Quebec. This offer is limited to one order per household. Not valid for current subscribers to Harlequin Heartwarming larger-print books. All orders subject to credit approval. Credit or debit balances in a customer's account(s) may be offset by any other outstanding balance owed by or to the customer. Please allow 4 to 6 weeks for delivery. Offer available while quantities last.

Your Privacy—The Harlequin® Reader Service is committed to protecting your privacy. Our Privacy Policy is available online at www.ReaderService.com or upon request from the Harlequin Reader Service.

We make a portion of our mailing list available to reputable third parties that offer products we believe may interest you. If you prefer that we not exchange your name with third parties, or if you wish to clarify or modify your communication preferences, please visit us at www.ReaderService.com/consumerchoice or write to us at Harlequin Reader Service Preference Service, P.O. Box 9062, Buffalo, NY 14269. Include your complete name and address.

HWDIR13R